The Wheel Turns

Also by Elizabeth Lemarchand

The Wheel Turns

ELIZABETH LEMARCHAND

WALKER AND COMPANY
NEW YORK

First published in the United States of America
in 1984 by the Walker Publishing Company, Inc.

Library of Congress Cataloging in Publication Data

Lemarchand, Elizabeth
  The wheel turns.

  I. Title.
PR6062.E5W48   1984   823'.914   84-13200
ISBN: 0-8027-5598-4

Printed in the United States of America

10 9 8 7 6 5 4 3 2 1

To Gwenda, Heather and Judy

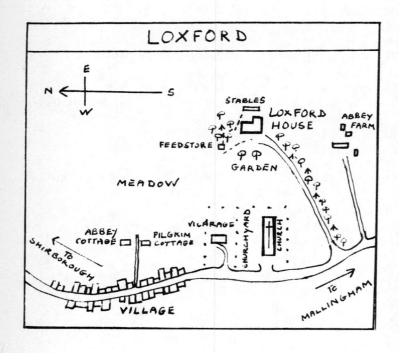

LOXFORD

CHIEF CHARACTERS

Basil Railsdon, widower, of Loxford House, Loxford
Amanda Railsdon, his daughter
Mrs Emily Bennett, his housekeeper
Henrietta Legge of Abbey Cottage, Loxford
The Reverend Martin Crabbe, Vicar of Loxford
Erica Crabbe, his wife
Jeremy Crabbe his son
Tom Whitworth of Abbey Farm, Loxford, tenant of
    Basil Railsdon
Bill Cobbledick, builder and undertaker
Laura Raymond, employee of Seabright's Superstore,
    Medstone, Surrey
Detective-Superintendent Gregg of the Crantshire
    C.I.D.
Detective-Inspector Blair
Detective-Chief Superintendent Tom Pollard of New
    Scotland Yard
Detective-Inspector Gregory Toye

ABBESS ARETÊ OVERTON – deceased

Chapter One

The Central Committee Rooms of the North Crantshire Conservative Association were packed to suffocation. The formal business of the meeting was over and the noise deafening: congratulations, back-slapping, roars of laughter and clinking of glasses. The occasion was the formal adoption of Basil Railsdon of Loxford House, Loxford, as the constituency's candidate at the next General Election. James Conibeer, the sitting Member, had decided to retire when the dissolution of the existing Parliament took place. He had represented North Crantshire for twenty-two years with an average majority of twenty thousand. It was a safe seat and had been much sought after. The final decision of the Selection Committee was that Basil Railsdon possessed the essential qualifications to an unusual degree. He lived in the constituency. Aged forty-two he was eminently presentable in person, wealthy, and already involved up to the hilt in local affairs. A widower of two years' standing, public opinion had already remarried him to Henrietta Legge, the sole survivor of an old Crantshire family, and obviously cut out to be the wife of an active M.P. She was thirty, attractive without being conventionally beautiful, and got on happily with

Amanda Railsdon, Basil's daughter and the only child of his first marriage.

The crowd began to thin out gradually.

'I've got to push off!' Basil Railsdon shouted in James Conibeer's rather deaf left ear. 'This razzamatazz of young Jeremy Crabbe's in Loxford church. You know.'

'Rum show,' the Member commented. 'Must be something in it or the Home Office would never have given an all-clear for opening up the grave. Bit of sharp practice by the Abbey people when old Henry the Eighth got going that young Crabbe's somehow got on to? Buried treasure, what?'

'Could be,' Basil Railsdon agreed as they made their way to the street door. 'Anyway, I thought it might be a good idea to turn up in case anything comes of it.'

'Quite right, my boy, quite right. First principle for a prospective constituency Member. Always be on the spot if anything's happening that could make the headlines. Take it from the old buffer.'

James Conibeer emptied his tankard in a parting gesture of farewell, slapped Basil on the back and returned to the Committee Rooms. Basil hurried across the road to the car park, unlocked his Hyperion and flung himself into the driving seat. Muttering imprecations he edged his way through the crowded streets of Shirborough, Crantshire's largest town and the headquarters of its local government and political parties. At the same time he had an underlying and intoxicated feeling of being swept along on the crest of a wave of success. He had not only inherited money but had made a good deal more through his various business interests. Loxford House, mainly eighteenth century but incorporating fragments of the former Abbey, could fairly be referred to by him as 'my place down in Crantshire'.

2

His first marriage had been marginally county at the price of dullness. Now, after a decent interval of two years, he was free to marry Henrietta Legge, who was indisputably county and young enough to give him a son. He was confident that she was poised to accept him, by now well over the death of her former fiancé, a young army officer killed some years earlier in a car crash. Moreover he had a flair for keeping his ear to the ground, and had learnt that the mounting pressure of inflation on a moderate fixed income had recently driven her to take out a mortgage on the attractive cottage in Loxford village that she had inherited from her parents. Obviously maintaining her social standing meant a great deal to her. His money and prospective political career would be irresistible . . .

On emerging at last from Shirborough, Basil Railsdon glanced at his watch. It was later than he thought, and a few miles beyond the town he was held up at road repairs. He decided to take a chance by turning off on to the old coast road which would cut off a couple of miles. It was rather narrow, but one was unlikely to meet a farm vehicle during the traditional twelve-to-one o'clock lunch hour. Bearing right he plunged between high, leafy hedges, driving fast. The road ran close to the cliff edge in a series of rises and falls and rounding a succession of bends. The imminence of a particularly blind one was indicated by a washed-out notice-board leaning at a drunken angle. Without much reducing speed he approached the corner on the wrong side of the road. Startled by the sudden appearance of the car a small girl who had climbed up on to the notice-board lost her grip and fell. She was struck by the bumper and flung into the air, crashing down head-first as Basil jammed on his brakes . . .

She was unmistakeably dead, her neck broken and

3

her head lolling. Her eyes stared in blank astonishment.

Swifter than through normal formulated thought, Basil understood that he was facing a charge of manslaughter, his political ambitions obliterated – his standing in the local community damaged beyond repair. Almost without conscious volition, self-protection took over. He lifted the small body and put it in the boot. Then he intently scrutinised the surface of the road for any sign of the accident. No blood. If she bled in the boot, that could be taken care of. Flinging himself into the driving seat again he started up the engine, his heart pounding and his mouth dry.

It was at the precise moment when the car moved forward that he got an impression from his driving mirror – too fleeting to carry conviction – of a car appearing at the crest of the rise behind him. He drove on quickly but carefully, hoping to get out on to the main road before any following car could get near enough to observe the Hyperion closely or, worse still, make a note of its number. Agonisingly, he was held up at the road junction, and sat staring into the mirror. But as the seconds passed no other car materialised behind him. His confidence began to return. It must have been imagination. The whole thing had been a bit of a shock, of course, and the appalling problem of how to dispose of the child's body lay ahead. However, he had always believed in the principle of one step at a time, and the important thing was to be alert to every conceivable opportunity that presented itself. At last there was a break in the procession of passing cars and he shot out on to the main Shirborough-Mallingham road and turned right. As long as he could he kept an eye on the driving mirror. No car emerged from the cliff road, and in a short time the first cottages of Loxford village came in sight, followed by the fine perpendicular tower of the former Abbey Church.

He drove into the gravelled sweep on the north side of the church. Several cars were already parked there. One, a Volvo with a London numberplate, was doubtless the property of the Home Office representative whose presence at the opening of the grave was required by law. A local police car was there, and the van owned by Bill Cobbledick, a Loxford builder who was also the village undertaker and in charge of the activities in progress inside the church. A fourth car was a battered Mini belonging to Jeremy Crabbe, the vicar's son. Presumably it had been decided to use the vestry door for all the comings and goings as less likely to attract attention than the more obvious south door nearer the road.

Basil Railsdon got out of the Hyperion and locked it. He was aware of being keyed up to top pitch, yet in some way exhilarated at the challenges ahead of him. He tried the boot of his car and satisfied himself that it was securely locked. He had a key to the vestry door but found it was ajar and went inside. This small annexe to the chancel contained the usual equipment of cassocks and surplices on hangers, a small wall-safe, a wooden table and sundry cupboards and chairs.

From the narrow priest's door leading to the chancel came the jarring impact of hammer on chisel in short sharp bursts, which returned in ghostly echo from the vaulted roof overhead. Minute particles of dust were hanging in the sunlight flooding through the south windows. In the brief intervals of silence terse comments were exchanged between Bill Cobbledick and his helpers who were on their knees round a gravestone let into the chancel floor. Scattered around them was a litter of chisels, hammers, chisel bars, rollers, webbing,

5

spades and a short ladder. Basil Railsdon's quick glance also registered the vicar, Martin Crabbe, deep in conversation with the diocesan architect at the west end of the church. There was presumably some structural or maintenance problem under discussion. There was something in Martin Crabbe's stance with his cassock hitched up on his left shoulder that suggested irritation. He was a stocky, determined man in his early sixties with red hair streaked with grey – dead against this whole business, Basil thought, and not surprisingly. Jeremy may very well be going to make a complete fool of himself, and the parish a butt for the papers and the media. He took a step forward and attracted the attention of three people talking together at the entrance to the chancel, and was taken aback at the pleasure he felt as Henrietta Legge broke away and came towards him. He raised a hand in greeting and a smile lit up her face.

'Not that I ever had any doubts about getting the permit,' she said, 'Not for a moment. Come and meet Mr Milton Travers from the Home Office.'

Milton Travers was somewhere in his mid-sixties, impeccably dressed in a dark suit and with an air of officialdom about him. He was pleasantly congratulatory to Basil, and expressed keen interest in the exhumation. Basil admitted to being a bit out of his depth.

'I'm not educated up to the level of all you people,' he said ruefully. 'And honestly, does it matter who was buried in that grave?'

'Well, it won't influence the course of history, I grant you,' Milton Travers replied, 'But it could turn out to be a masterly piece of documentary detective work by young Mr Crabbe, and could tell us a bit more about the sort of thing that went on at the time of the Dissolution, a period of social disintegration in some respects rather suggestive of the present day. It must be most intriguing for you, Miss Legge,' he went on, turning to Henrietta. 'Your forebears actually gave this church to the parish, didn't they?'

He saw that his knowledge of the fact pleased her.

'That's right, Mr Travers,' she replied, 'although we always think it wasn't quite the grand gesture it sounds. Loxford Abbey was a small foundation with poor endowments, and Henry the Eighth's Commission took such a dim view of it that once they'd stripped the lead off the roofs they sold off the buildings as a job lot to my up-and-coming ancestors. My own view is that the family saw in it a sort of investment in Lord of the Manor status.'

'What happened to the rest of the Abbey?' Milton Travers asked.

'It became a handy stone quarry for the neighbourhood,' Basil Railsdon told him. 'You come across chunks of the stone built into houses and cottages and sheds all over the village. There's quite a lot of it in my place, including a rather fine fireplace. I suppose I can't persuade you to change your mind and let me put you up for the night?'

'Would that I could, but I've got a committee early tomorrow morning, and I'm hoping to get off in good time to do a spot of homework before going to bed. If you'll excuse me I'll go and see how your chaps are getting on.'

He gave Henrietta a formal little bow and walked into the chancel.

'Let's park in this front pew,' Basil said to her. 'We can see when they get the stone up.'

Henrietta settled herself at a nicely-adjudged distance from him, and put down her handbag beside her. Basil manoeuvred himself as comfortably as he could into the corner of the pew, kicked away a hassock and crossed his legs.

'How did it go?' she asked.

'Like a bomb. Actually it had been settled *sub rosa* a couple of days ago, and I knew last night, but old Connie made me swear to keep mum.'

'I'm absolutely thrilled,' Henrietta said. 'Quite apart from everything else, you're so patently the man for the job. All the local links as well as your wider contacts.'

'Bless you for that. At the moment I've got that ghastly new boy feeling in the pit of my stomach. And it won't exactly help if Jeremy Crabbe starts off by making the place a laughing stock over this grave business. Can't you see the gutter press headings? "*Home Office Permit to Open Empty Tomb.*". "*Unburied Treasure Farce in Village Church.*" '

'And, of course, bang goes that Junior Research Fellowship he's up for.'

'That would be the one advantage. Without the money he can't afford to marry Amanda unless I subsidise her. Damn it, Henrietta, I want a better match for her than a history master in a second-rank public school, even if the chap's unquestionably got brains and is getting stuff he's edited into egg-head journals.'

He glanced up to meet laughter in her fine, deep blue eyes, and appreciated the personality and breeding in her face that more than compensated for the absence of unquestioned beauty. Steps were approaching from behind, and they turned to see Martin Crabbe and the diocesan surveyor bearing down on them armed with notebooks.

*　　　*　　　*

8

On entering the chancel, Milton Travers paused for a word with P.C. Ford of the Crantshire Constabulary whose presence, like his own, was required by law, and went on to speak to Bill Cobbledick who was superintending the manoeuvering of a roller under the gravestone, a large rectangular slab of the local sandstone measuring roughly three feet by five. Originally a pale buff in colour, it had darkened over the passage of four centuries. The brief inscription had been roughly and deeply incised and was clearly legible:

A deep crack had developed running from side to side under the lettering. Bill Cobbledick looked up as Milton Travers approached, pulling off a pair of goggles worn to protect his eyes from dust and splinters. His face, red from exertion, was weatherbeaten, and his eyes were intelligent and alert behind old-fashioned steel-rimmed spectacles, the bridge of which cut deeply into his nose.

'Never ought to have 'appened,' he said, indicating the crack. 'Not a chance o' getting 'er up in one piece.'

'But you'll fill it in with mortar when you replace the stone, I take it?' Milton Travers suggested. 'It won't be so noticeable then.'

'That it won't, Sir, not if we're careful with the colour. Here's my nevvy Walt with another roller from the van. We don't want no more cracks developin'.'

A lad with a marked resemblance to Bill came through the vestry and responded inarticulately to Milton Travers' greeting.

'How deep do you expect the grave to be, Mr Cobbledick?' the latter asked.

9

'Not above six feet, Sir. They didn't have all the regulations in those days that we've got now.'

'Won't the sides have caved in?'

'Seein' it was a grave for an Abbess I'd expect them to 'ave lined it with brick, and one or two o' they could've dropped down, but not to do much harm. And I'd think they'd put away a lady in her position in lead.'

'Well, I mustn't hold you up,' Milton Travers said, and moved off. He went over to the choir stalls on the decanal side, where Jeremy Crabbe was watching the workman with rapt attention.

'May I join you?' he asked.

Jeremy scrambled to his feet and revealed himself as a rather leggy young man in slacks and an open-necked shirt. He had an intelligent, enquiring face and auburn hair worn on the long side.

'Sorry, Sir,' he said. 'I didn't register that it was you talking to Bill. Come and sit here. It's a good vantage point and I'll move along a bit.'

'Rather a moment in your life, isn't it?' Milton Travers asked as he settled himself.

'It's sheer hell, actually.' Jeremy Crabbe sat bolt upright, gripping the book ledge in front of him with both hands. 'What sort of a fool am I going to look if, after all, Bill does unearth "female remains", as he calls them, and my theory of Aretê Overton's burial here being a fake is blown sky-high? Just when I'm going up to Oxford to be interviewed for a Junior Research Fellowship at Athanasius. There's not a hope of keeping it quiet. There's been a leak somehow. I've been up to the top of the tower and had a look round. There are two blokes draped with cameras hanging about.'

'Well, well,' Milton Travers commented. 'Athanasius. My own college, as it happens. Let's look at your

10

prospects from the opposite point of view. An empty grave here might clinch that Fellowship, you know. Of course I've read that excellent report you submitted to the Home Office, but it must have been selective to some extent. Fill me in a bit about your fascination with the past.'

'Well, for some reason I got hooked on early history as soon as I could read. Cavemen and whatever. At school I got the same kick out of prehistory and early history as my peers were getting out of science-fiction. They thought I was dotty, of course, but fortunately my games were O.K. so I kept my head above water. Then Dad being a cleric helped. Masses of books in the house that had been handed down the family. The history teaching at both my schools was good, and I managed to pick up a history scholarship and a First. But the top thrill was when I was about ten and discovered that one could get at the raw material of a history text-book oneself. That there were genuine antiquities and valid documents in existence. Then, just before I went up to Oxford, my father accepted this living, and hardly anywhere could have been more up my street. The cartulary of Loxford Abbey is unusually complete and I soon got on to it in the P.R.O. Several of the abbesses' tombs are in this church, and I managed to check the dates and identify "AO" – he indicated the grave that was being opened – with Aretê Overton, the last abbess but one. It was her successor who surrendered the house to Henry's Commissioners in 1536. From the start I was intrigued by the name "Aretê".'

'Aretê,' Milton Travers murmured reflectively. 'That untranslatable Greek word for the essence of excellence. What sort of family did she come from?'

'This is it, sir. They were quite undistinguished country people, farming a small estate about thirty miles

11

from here. One or two were J.P.s, but that seems to be as far as they got in public life. None of them appears to have been to Oxford or Cambridge. The only faint clue is a battered crusader tomb in their parish church reported to be that of an Overton, but I haven't been able to find any confirmation of this. And, maddeningly, the family died out in the eighteenth century.'

'Unfortunate, that. Most families pass down a few records and bits and pieces. Do carry on.'

'Well, the next development was the utterly fantastic stroke of luck I had at a small town called Hollowdale in the Border Country . . .'

Jeremy Crabbe described how he had been driving south from a visit to relatives in Scotland and passed an advance notice of a turn-off to Hollowdale. He remembered reading about some unusually fine mediaeval glass in its parish church, and decided that he could spare the time to go and have a look at it. He had met the vicar as he walked round, who, as well as pointing out features of special interest in the glass, had shown him a transcript of the parish registers. These had been kept from the unusually early date of 1539.

'He just opened it at random near the beginning, and by pure chance my eye fell on a 1546 burial entry. It was *"Aretê Overton aetat 54 pilgrime from afarre"*. You know, I still wake up in the night and wonder if I dreamt the whole thing . . .'

'I can put your mind at rest on that score,' Milton Travers told him. 'When the Home Office got your application for a permit to open the grave here we sent a chap up to Hollowdale to check the entry in the register.'

Jeremy grinned. 'In my saner moments I realise that you would have done that before anything else.'

12

'It was the coincidence of the dates that we found remarkable. We vetted the Loxford cartulary at the P.R.O. too, of course, and it states categorically that Aretê was elected Abbess in 1520 at the age of thirty. According to the gravestone here she was buried in 1528 at the age of thirty-eight. The Hollowdale register of burials records her death in 1546 aged fifty-six. Tell me, assuming that her funeral here was a fake, have you formed any theory about the whole extraordinary business?'

'The only thing that I can think of is that the Overtons in some way got across the powers that be, although it's difficult to imagine how, in view of their modest status and lifestyle. Some of the smaller religious houses were being closed in the early 1520s, and possibly the Loxford community thought they'd have a better chance of survival without an Overton as Abbess. But I haven't found the slightest trace of anything of this sort in any of the records, or any link between the Overtons and the Hollowdale district.'

'You could conceivably be on to something, all the same,' Milton Travers said thoughtfully. 'I wonder if . . .'

His speculation was drowned by a series of grating sounds accompanied by shouts enjoining caution from Bill Cobbledick. A small cloud of dust rose from the area of the grave.

''Er's shifted, Vicar!' Bill proclaimed triumphantly in the direction of the nave.

*   *   *

The stark, dark rectangle of the grave, no longer decently camouflaged by the stone slab, had an unexpectedly chilling effect on the little group of spectators

13

who at once gathered round hastily and then kept their distance. Basil Railsdon stood immobilised by the possibility that had suddenly occurred to him. Only Jeremy took a couple of steps forward, hands hanging at his sides and tightly clenched, while his father and Bill Cobbledick peered into the depths with the help of a powerful electric torch. After what seemed an interminable period, Bill straightened up.

'There's no coffin, and not a sign of remains laid down there in a shroud', he said. 'Look for yourself, Vicar. Never used for a burial this grave wasn't. Air just a bit musty when we opened up, but no more. Mr Jeremy's a rare one for ferrettin' things out. Shall us get up what looks to be a small box up the top end?'

'Just a moment,' Milton Travers said, coming forward with a camera. 'I want a photograph for the official record.'

It was agreed that Jeremy should go down and retrieve the box-like object. Bill Cobbledick held things up for a few minutes while he examined the brick lining of the grave to see if any shoring-up was necessary. Jeremy, in the hour of his triumph, became authoritative.

'Whatever this object is it's got to be handled with great care,' he said. 'If it's a wooden box, for instance, it could disintegrate on being suddenly exposed to the air after being shut away underground for four centuries.'

The ladder was set up and he made a cautious descent. After a few moments his voice came up hollowly.

'I want a large cloth of some sort so that I can make a sling to bring the thing up in.'

'I'll get you a dust-sheet from the cleaner's cupboard,' Henrietta called back.

In due course Jeremy's head appeared over the

edge of the grave, and he was helped on to *terra firma* carrying something in an old sheet with the four corners knotted together. This was carefully placed on a small table fetched from the vestry. Jeremy untied the knots and let the sheet fall to reveal a box roughly two feet square, and wrapped in what appeared to be a kind of coarse linen, grey with age, unpleasantly speckled with the mould of decay and giving off a musty odour.

An exceedingly macabre development followed. The wrapping began to move. It trembled, began to disintegrate, and silently collapsed on to the table, exposing a tarnished metal box. As it subsided round the base of the box tiny clouds of dust arose, some settling on the sheet and some sinking to the floor. Unconsciously the spectators had drawn a little closer together. Milton Travers relieved the tension by advancing purposefully with his camera.

'Has anybody got a clean envelope?' Jeremy asked. 'I want to take some samples of the dust for analysis.'

'I'll get some spare Christian Stewardship ones from the safe,' Basil Railsdon said quickly, and vanished into the vestry.

'You're up in this sort of thing, aren't you?' Martin Crabbe asked Milton Travers. 'Is there anything special about the box as far as you can see at this stage?'

'From the shape and size I rather think it's a casket for carrying alleged relics in processions. Shall I try to open it?'

'Yes, do.'

The box was locked. He turned it over carefully. There was a small sound as a little key became detached from the base and fell on to the table.

'That's a bit of luck,' he said, 'assuming it fits.'

'I reckon a drop of oil couldn't do no harm,' Bill Cobbledick suggested, producing a small oil can.

15

By common consent Jeremy inserted the key. It turned with surprisingly little difficulty. The hinges were stiff, but after treatment with oil allowed the lid of the box to be raised with a grating noise. Milton Travers displayed uncharacteristic animation.

'What I hoped we'd find!' he exclaimed. From the crumbled padded lining of the box he extracted a crystal cylinder mounted in a holder of tarnished metal like that of the box itself, and with a stem running down to a circular base. He stood it on the table.

'The crystal's a bit cloudy after all this time,' he said as everyone crowded round. 'But if you look closely – just here – you can see the actual relic. That tiny fragment of frayed darkish material was possibly revered as part of the Virgin's robe, as the Abbey was dedicated to St Mary.'

'Is this sort of thing valuable?' Basil Railsdon asked, peering at the casket with interest.

'It *can* be extremely valuable,' Milton Travers replied. 'This casket is undoubtedly Islamic work: I should put it tentatively at somewhere between the eighth and tenth centuries. The ornamentation is typically geometrical, isn't it?', he said, turning to Jeremy. 'That vague tradition that one of the Overtons went on a crusade may have something in it. That disgraceful business in 1204, for instance, when the Venetians sacked Constantinople.'

Jeremy, who was showing unmistakeable signs of exhilaration, agreed enthusiastically.

'The Overtons might have been hard up when Aretê was elected Abbess, and decided to let the Abbey have the casket and reliquary as a sort of celebration present. Then, if it was decided that she'd better fade out temporarily, the Abbey might have decided to try to hang on to it.'

16

Bill Cobbledick cleared his throat vigorously.

'All this talk's beyond me,' he said. 'What I want to know is who these 'ere things belongs to. Are they Crown property as 'tis called, or property o' this parish? As People's Warden I wants to know.'

'They're certainly not Crown property,' Martin Crabbe replied. 'Don't you remember that at my induction the Bishop put me in possession of the church building and all property connected with it, to hold on behalf of the parish of Loxford? My duty now is to have these undoubtedly valuable things removed to a safe place and examined by official experts. The Cathedral Treasury seems to . . .'

'Hell!' Jeremy burst in. 'One of those newshounds has climbed up somehow and he's snooping through the east window.'

As he spoke there was a vigorous pounding on the south door, and demands in a powerful masculine voice to open up.

'Broadbent,' Jeremy and his father exchanged glances. 'Assistant Editor of the *North Crantshire Evening News*', Martin Crabbe explained. 'How these chaps get onto things in the way they do I simply can't think.'

Milton Travers and Basil Railsdon, both with considerable experience of the publicity techniques of press and media, advised cooperation with Mr Broadbent.

'Better to let them have the correct facts to start with,' Milton Travers urged, to the accompaniment of a further fusillade of knocks.

Jim Broadbent was a personality, short and stocky with a red face and impertinent blue eyes, but appeared momentarily taken aback by the size of his reception party. He was clearly impressed on being introduced to Milton Travers as the official representative of the Home Office.

'We caught a sniff of something a bit out of the ordinary going on up here,' he said, 'so I thought I'd come along on spec . . . Good God!' he exclaimed, catching sight of the open grave, 'Who's being dug up?'

'I think we'd better put you in the picture, Jim.' Martin Crabbe said. 'Let's go and sit down. Your photographer can get cracking as long as he doesn't get in anybody's way.'

The workmen had retreated to the grave where they were engaged in examining the soil at the bottom, and pointedly ignored the interested press photographer. At a conference in the south aisle Jeremy held his own under intensive fire from Jim Broadbent, supported by Milton Travers and Basil Railsdon, the latter subtly emphasising his status as prospective parliamentary candidate for the constituency.

'Well,' Jim Broadbent said finally, 'I've heard some rum yarns in my time, but this one tops the lot. We'll beat it back to Shirborough hell for leather, and see what we can do with the front page of tomorrow's *News*. The media'll beat us to it, of course, but in my opinion folk like to see things down in black and white and read them half-a-dozen times, and then post 'em off to Auntie Flo in Australia . . . Come on Smith,' he bellowed. 'Sorry, Vicar. Forgot I was in a sacred edifice.'

The church seemed large, empty and silent as the door slammed behind the press party. Jeremy came down from the chancel.

'If you'd like to take the casket into Mallingham right now, Dad,' he said, 'Basil says he'll drive you and the bobby will provide a police escort. I'll bring up the rear and drop off at school. I ought to get back as soon as possible: they've been jolly decent to me about time off over this business, and I'm due in Oxford tomorrow night.'

18

Martin Crabbe glanced at his watch.

'Right,' he said. 'Your mother will be back from her committee by now. Just tell her very briefly what's happened and what I'm doing and ask her to ring up the Archdeacon. He's expecting a call. I'll get back as soon as I possibly can.'

'O.K.', Jeremy replied, and disappeared into the vestry.

'Regretfully,' Milton Travers said, 'I must get off, too. This affair has been a highlight in my normally rather pedestrian job. I hope you'll keep me posted.'

'We most certainly will,' Martin Crabbe assured him. 'Goodbye, and many thanks for all your support.'

Bill Cobbledick and his helpers were knocking off, grouping their equipment in orderly fashion for the next morning. The lower section of the gravestone had been manoeuvered back into place, and a plank was laid across the still open area as a token security measure. Martin Crabbe congratulated them warmly on having carried through the whale of a job so successfully.

'It's been interestin',' Bill Cobbledick conceded. 'Us'll finish off easy tomorrow, mortarin' an' all. Thank you, Sir,' he added, as Basil Railsdon slipped a pound note into his hand, and suggested that the Ring of Bells was only just round the corner, and on everybody's way home.

'All ready,' Henrietta Legge said, who had been securely parcelling up the casket and reliquary against any possible hazards on the journey.

Basil took the package from her, and the three of them went out together. Martin Crabbe selected a key from the bunch on his ring and locked the outer door of the vestry. Henrietta was invited to make the trip too, but declined.

19

'Many thanks, but I think I'm for home,' she said. 'It's been quite a day, hasn't it?'

She waved off the Hyperion as it rounded the east end of the church.

*   *   *

It was nearly three hours later when Basil Railsdon drew up at the front door of the Loxford Vicarage. Erica Crabbe appeared at the top of the steps. As the two men greeted her with apologies for their lateness Martin caught sight of her face in the light of the porch lamp.

'Anything wrong?' he asked, leaping out of the car, a sequence of dire possibilities rushing through his mind.

Erica Crabbe in her late fifties was still good-looking, with dark, curly hair worn short and a pleasant, if determined face, at the moment clouded.

'Yes,' she told him, 'It's little Pippa Cobbledick, Bill's grandchild. She's been missing since some time, after eleven this morning from the holiday camp where she was staying with her parents.'

'Some time after eleven?' echoed Martin incredulously. 'Why on earth didn't the parents get on to Bill and his wife sooner? He obviously knew nothing about it up to a short time ago.'

'The usual explanation of a situation like this: a misunderstanding and a muddle. There are a lot of young families at this holiday camp place just off the Shirborough-Loxford road and it was arranged for some parents, including Pippa's, to have a day off while other families looked after their children. Round about tea-time it was discovered that there were two families, each of which thought Pippa had been with the other since lunch. The police have been called in, of

20

course. When I heard Basil's car I thought it might be some news.'

'Where is this holiday camp?' Basil Railsdon asked, joining the other two on the steps.

'It belongs to a farm on the Shirborough-Mallingham road, about a mile on the Loxford side of where the old cliff road goes off on the right. The camp is in a field on the sea side of the farm.'

'I came along the old road this morning as it's a short-cut, and I was raring to get back to the church here. But I didn't see a sign of any kids, either in a group or one on its own. How old is this grandchild of Bill's?'

'Three, I think. Rising four, I should say.'

'I don't like this at all,' Martin Crabbe said in a worried voice. 'She's old enough to wander off on her own, and could easily have got across the old road and the strip of rough grass and gorse on the far side, and taken a header over the cliffs.'

'That's right,' his wife replied. 'The police and the coastguard have been searching the rocks below, but unfortunately it was high tide at half-past three, before the search got going. And there's another thing,' she went on, ruffling her hair, 'People have been listening to all the news bulletins and announcements, and the police want anybody who was on either of the two roads between eleven and four today to contact them. Would you like to ring from here, Basil, and share the steak casserole that's in the oven, or would you rather go home and phone from there?'

'It's awfully good of you, Erica, but Benny will have been keeping something hot for me for hours, and I think it would be tactful to go home and consume it. I'll ring you back later or come along if anything crops up from my phone call to the police.'

21

When he had driven off, the Crabbes went into the vicarage kitchen.

'My guess is that he'll find a telephone message from Amanda waiting for him,' Erica said, as she spooned out stewed steak and assorted vegetables. 'She rang here about half-an-hour ago thinking she might catch him with us. Jeremy had already phoned her about the grave and the casket. She said her exams ended at mid-day tomorrow, and she was catching an evening plane and wanted her father to meet her at Heathrow. She's taking the Research Fellowship for granted now, of course.'

'And I suppose we take their engagement for granted. Amanda's nineteen and of age, and Basil can't stop the marriage. Quite apart from what Jeremy earns, she comes into her mother's money when she's twenty . . . Oh dear! I do hate strained relations with people, and if Basil's really hostile it's bound to take the edge off their happiness.'

Erica agreed. 'I can't make up my mind whether he wants Amanda to marry a man who's going to make his mark, as he once said to me, for her own sake or for the reflected glory for himself.'

'I'm pretty sure he's never faced that one,' Martin replied, 'or that the question's ever occurred to him, come to that. One thing must be dealt with: getting the church presentable to open during tomorrow. As soon as . . .'

'Hold it,' Erica broke in. 'I forgot for the moment to say that when Bill rang to tell me what had happened, he said he'd contacted Tom Moss and told him to get the second bit of the gravestone back first thing tomorrow with Walt's help. He says they can cope perfectly well, and will call for the vestry key soon after eight. But he'd like the mortaring left to do himself.

22

Even with the worry over the child he's upset at having to leave the job in the middle.'

'Dependable as a rock . . . I must say I'm grateful not to have to go round the village tonight trying to fix things up myself. It's been quite a day.'

Basil Railsdon rang not long afterwards to say that the Shirborough police had been glad to have the information about his having been on the cliff road that morning, but that there was no fresh news. On hearing of the arrangement for Tom Moss and Walt White to finish putting back the gravestone the next morning he expressed relief.

'God knows how long poor old Bill will be out of action,' he said, 'and people are bound to turn up and go gooping round the church after all the publicity. Well, let's call it a day, shall we? There seems to have been rather a lot of it.'

He rang off. Erica, who had been following on the extension in the vicarage kitchen, came into the study.

'I'd lay a modest bet that Amanda *has* rung him about coming home tomorrow, but he didn't want to discuss it with us now.'

'Don't blame him,' her husband said with a gigantic yawn.

Chapter Two

On the following morning Basil Railsdon slit open and sorted his post over breakfast at Loxford House. At the sound of wheels on the gravel drive, he looked up to see a panda car pass the window and draw up at the front door.

He got up quickly, summoning his normal cheerful and confident expression, and went out into the hall. A spruce, pleasant-looking police officer introduced himself as Detective-Inspector Blair of the county C.I.D., proffering his official card.

'We're grateful to you, Sir, for ringing us so promptly last night,' he said. 'I've brought along your statement, if you'd kindly run your eye over it, and sign it if you agree that it's accurate. And there are one or two other points where we hope you might be able to help us.'

'I only hope I can,' Basil replied, 'but I rather doubt it, I'm afraid. Do I take it that there's still no news of the little girl?'

'I'm afraid not, Sir, although we started on an intensive search again at first light.'

Basil led the way to his study, offered Inspector Blair a chair, and sat down at his desk to read the typewritten version of the information he had given the police over the telephone the night before.

'*This morning, Wednesday, May the fifteenth,*' he had told them, '*I was driving in my Hyperion from Shirborough to Loxford, after my adoption meeting as prospective Conservative candidate for the constituency. The process had taken longer than I had expected, and I had an appointment here in Loxford, so I took the short-cut along the old cliff road which saves about two miles. I saw no one at any point on this road. I cannot be absolutely exact about timing, but it was twelve-thirty-five by the church clock at Little Woodford as I drove through the village after I rejoined the main road.*'

'I'm afraid there's nothing I can add to this, Inspector,' he said, handing back the typescript.

'There's just one other point we might have raised with you last night, Sir. I expect you were held up briefly when you did rejoin the main road?'

'Yes, I was. For about half-a-minute or so, I should think. It had started to rain, and people were slowing down a bit.'

'You didn't by any chance notice a small girl with an adult or adults in any of the cars that went past?'

'No, I'm quite sure I didn't. It was mainly commercial traffic.'

'And you didn't at any time notice a car coming along the cliff road behind you in your driving mirror?'

'No. And no car came up behind me when I was waiting to get out on to the main road.'

'Thank you, Sir. That clears up all my points nicely.'

Inspector Blair added the information to the end of the typewritten statement which Basil Railsdon then signed and returned to him.

'If the poor little kid had gone over the cliff it would be preferable to some devil having enticed her away,' Basil remarked.

'Just what I feel about it myself, Sir, but we've made

the most exhaustive search of that bit of beach and the rocks, and there isn't a trace of her. Not a shoe, for instance, or a bit of clothing . . . Well, I must get on and try my luck with the next one on the list of people who rang in.'

Basil went back into the house, finished sorting his correspondence and took it into his study. After a few moments' thought he picked up the telephone receiver and dialled the vicarage number.

'Loxford Vicarage,' Martin Crabbe's voice answered with distinct abruptness . . . 'Oh, sorry, Basil. I didn't know it was you, of course. I'm being driven up the wall by calls from the press and T.V. people.'

Basil commiserated. 'I've just had a police inspector here,' he said, 'A very decent chap. He wanted me to sign the statement I gave them over the line last night. No doubt you know already that there's absolutely no news. What I really rang about was to ask if there's anything I can do to help down at church this morning. I've got to go up to Town after lunch and shan't be back until pretty late. Amanda's rung to say she finishes her diploma exams this morning and has suddenly decided to fly back on an evening plane. She'll have a mountain of luggage, of course, and I simply must go up and meet her. Really, the way the young expect their parents to dance attendance on them these days . . .'

'Awfully good of you to offer,' Martin replied. 'Walt White and young Moss are already on to the job of getting the second bit of the gravestone back. They seem sure they can cope after all the practice they had with the rollers yesterday. I've told them to leave the mortaring for Bill. I know he wants to finish off the job, poor chap, come what may. Less hope every hour of Pippa turning up safe and sound, let's face it. Then Mrs Mandle's started on her usual weekend clean-up now. I

26

think I'd better stay here for the moment and cope with the phone calls. And I'm doing a notice to put up on the south door saying that the casket and its contents are in the care of the Cathedral authorities, and not, repeat NOT, in the church. Henrietta's taking down fresh flowers, and everything ought to be looking presentable by this afternoon. If you could just drop in and say a few encouraging words it would brace everyone up, I think, but otherwise the situation's under control.'

'I'll certainly do that thing. I want to put a couple of cheques for the Tower Appeal in the safe anyway. Right. I hope you won't have a lot more trouble with the newshounds.'

He rang off, and sat for a few moments resting his forehead on the palm of his left hand, reviewing the conversation. The information about Amanda's precipitate return had gone over quite casually and her matrimonial prospects were a secondary consideration. What did matter was an opportunity to replace unobserved the spare key to the outer door of the vestry which he had taken from its hook when fetching the Christian Stewardship envelopes for Jeremy, having suddenly seen a possible solution to his urgent problem: the foolproof disposal of Pippa Cobbledick's body. Here too, Basil felt, things were going his way. It was hardly credible that Walt White and Tom Moss, preoccupied with sudden and unexpected responsibility, would have given a glance at the row of keys hanging in the vestry. The same applied to Mrs Mandle whose cleaning equipment was kept in a cupboard at the north-west end of the church, together with the flower vases which Henrietta might possibly want. In fact, the only possibly worrying feature of the situation was that the mortaring was being left for Bill Cobbledick to do when he eventually came home. It really hinged on whether White and Moss had put back the piece of gravestone competently –. Of course, Bill's reaction would depend to a large extent on what had happened to the child. He would almost certainly be too shaken by what could only be a catastrophe to bother himself unduly about a trifle like the alignment of the bloody gravestone. But if, on the other hand, he insisted on taking it up again . . .

The coolheadedness which had stood Basil Railsdon in such good stead in a number of very big business deals returned to him. He even felt a certain sense of excitement at facing a major hazard. He collected the two cheques, went round to the garage behind the house for his car, and drove down to the church. Once again he parked next to the Cobbledicks' van and walked into the vestry. As he passed the row of hooks on which various keys were hung, his hand went out and noiselessly replaced the key of the outer door of the vestry, and he passed on into the church. The next moment he was in the chancel, and released an unconsciously pent-up breath. The stone had been faultlessly manoeuvered into position, and he was congratulating Walt White and Tom Moss on a first-class job.

' 'Twasn't all that difficult, Sir,' Walt said. 'Not after all the practice we'd had with the other bit and the rollers. Slipped in nicely, it did. We're to leave the finishin' off with mortar for Uncle Bill when 'e comes back, Vicar says. 'E was so set on gettin' jus' the right colour as wouldn't show.'

'Poor chap,' Tom Moss commented. 'If they don't find young Pippa safe an' sound, there'll be little enough we'll be able to do for Bill for a good long time to come. Worships that child, 'e does . . . Well, reckon we're through here now, so we'll collect up the bits an' pieces and be off. There's jobs enough with Bill away.'

'I must push off, too,' Basil said. 'I've got to drive up to London and collect my daughter from Heathrow. But I'd

28

better just pass the time of day with Mrs Mandle first, though.'

Mrs Mandle was small, dumpy and garrulous. As she saw Basil approaching her eyes lit up. She stopped her activities with a broom, and almost before he could bid her good morning embarked on a breathless commentary on the events of the past twenty-four hours. Eventually he managed to extricate himself, satisfied that she had not given a thought to the vestry key. Vicar had called early to ask her to change her day because of all the dust over everything after the grave was opened, and told her that he was letting in Walt White and Tom Moss by the vestry door, and she'd be able to get in too. When everything had been put to rights they'd open up the south door as usual, he'd said.

As Vicar's Warden, Basil had a key to the safe, and was just locating it among the others on his key ring when he heard footsteps on the gravel outside. The outer door opened and Henrietta Legge appeared on the threshold. She was wearing a light summer frock and carrying an armful of madonna lilies and delphiniums.

'Hallo!' Basil smiled at her. 'All out of your garden?' In a flash his quick mind had dressed her more formally and expensively, and had placed her at his side on a platform at a local Conservative Association gathering of some sort at which the Member's wife had been presented with a bouquet.

'Yes,' she said. 'They're doing well this summer. Martin thinks there'll be public interest in the church after yesterday, and wants it looking as natty as possible.'

'Two more cheques for the Tower Appeal have come in,' he said. 'We're over £14,200 now. Let's hope that public interest will encourage people to drop something

29

into the box . . . You haven't heard any news, I suppose?'

Henrietta shook her head. 'I've come through the village and there's absolutely none, apparently. I looked in on Bill's old mother, but mercifully she hasn't really taken it all in, according to the neighbours.'

'Good of you to go and see her,' he said, re-locking the safe – The right instincts for an M.P.'s wife, too – . For a wild moment he teetered on the brink of proposing to Henrietta then and there, but resisted the impulse. There was one more important matter to deal with before he could take the normality of life for granted. 'I rang Martin this morning, apologising for having to go up to Town after lunch when there's so much to cope with here, but he says everything's under control as far as the church goes. Amanda's finishing her exams this morning and flying back on a five-thirty plane. Draw your own conclusions.'

Henrietta, who was beginning to feel occasional anxious qualms at Basil's delay in making the proposal that was so widely expected, resisted the temptation to be a yes-woman.

'As I've remarked before,' she said with the faintest nuance of mockery, 'a distinguished academic son-in-law could be quite something, you know.'

He grimaced at her, and she knew that she had struck the right note.

'We don't know yet if he's landed this Fellowship affair. Probably shan't for weeks. Oxbridge isn't exactly geared to high speed. Well, I'm off. See you tomorrow.'

Henrietta listened to the car being started up and felt a return of confidence.

Driving round the east end of the church brought back to Basil the events of the previous night with disconcerting vividness. He deliberately relived them, convinced that this was the most effective way of exorcising the memories . . .

As part of the original Abbey buildings, the Loxford church stood a little beyond the village houses, surrounded on its north, south and east sides by an open space contained by a wall and bordered by trees and shrubs. After leaving Martin Crabbe about to have a belated supper at the vicarage, he had driven back to the church. There had been no one in sight as he turned in and parked the car out of sight from the road behind the east end. It was dark, apart from the light of a bright moon in a cloudless sky.

The first step had been simple: unlocking the vestry door with the spare key. Looking into the church he saw that the moonlight streaming through the south windows would make only very limited use of his torch necessary. In any case it was barely dark. A plank had been placed across the open section of the grave. He noted its position carefully and removed it. The short ladder was lying nearby, as he had observed when leaving the church earlier in the evening.

Listening intently at the open door of the vestry he had then returned to the car and unlocked the boot. Nearly twelve hours' confinement in a small, hot space had resulted in rigor already beginning to pass off. The little head was loose on the broken neck, and he had had to support it with his hand. The feel of the hair came disagreeably back to him now. Once inside the vestry he relocked the door and carried Pippa's inert form into the chancel.

He had already realised that lack of space would be his main difficulty. He lowered the body into the open section of the grave, as close to the broken edge of the

31

covering stone as possible. Then he had placed the ladder as far away from it as he could and climbed down. On his hands and knees he pushed the body to the far end of the covered area, and arranged it to occupy as little space as possible. Climbing up again he had cautiously directed the beam of a powerful torch downwards, and felt more satisfied than he had dared to hope . . . There was some risk involved, of course, but White and Moss would be anxious to get on with replacing the other section of the gravestone, and unlikely to waste any time examining the grave itself. He had felt a sudden urge to get out into the open air, and after very carefully restoring the ladder and plank to the positions in which he had found them, he had quietly let himself out of the vestry door and returned to his car.

The hazard now was that the car might be seen emerging from the church area at so unusual an hour. There had been a marvellous sense of release as he cautiously emerged into an empty road. As he was doing now, at this moment, in broad daylight, with the grave completely covered over . . .

The nightmare memories were fading rapidly. With an enormous sense of relief he headed for home, raising a hand to greet an acquaintance passing in a car towards the village. A few moments later he turned into the drive gates of Loxford House and came to a halt outside the porch. There was just one more precautionary job to do but he decided to deal with his morning's post first. Only a couple of congratulatory letters had managed to arrive so far. All such would have to be answered, but there was no urgency. The rest of his post was business correspondence and needed some attention. He was an efficient typist, but as his fingers flew over the keys he reflected with satisfaction that

32

secretarial help was to be laid on for him at Shirbor-ough for half-a-day a week to start with, increasing as required. Go about and see people, address meetings and whatever, but become a desk-hack, no. He stamped his correspondence and put it out on the hall table to be collected by the postman when the second delivery was brought. On the rare occasions when there was no mail for Loxford House, Mrs Bennett would see that the letters went down to the village post office. She was an absolute treasure of a housekeeper, he thought, as he strolled towards the kitchen. Worth every penny of the very handsome wage he paid her.

'Benny,' he said, going in to find her about to put an appetising-looking quiche into the oven, 'Let me have a dustpan and brush, will you? I brought home some plants in the boot of the car the other day, and there's a bit of spilt earth left behind. Amanda's sure to come back with a lot of coats and whatever that'll have to be got on board somehow.'

Mrs Bennett tut-tutted, offered to do the job herself and finally produced the dustpan and brush. So armed, Basil subjected the boot to an exhaustive inspection, sweeping it thoroughly after removing a rubber mat. This would have to be replaced, but for the moment it could be rolled up and dropped over some convenient bridge on the way to London, pristine though it appeared. He emptied the dustpan and returned it to the kitchen, where he learnt that his light luncheon would be on the table in a quarter of an hour.

On the London road he could sense normality and security returning to life with every mile. Drawing up in a lay-by close to a river he strolled to the nearby bridge and stood with his elbows on the parapet, the typical bird- or fish-watcher just having a short break on a long drive. At an opportune moment he let the rubber mat fall. It landed in midstream, and began to sink slowly as the current carried it away.

He was some miles further on when he was suddenly struck by the advantages that would accrue from proposing to Henrietta on his return and marrying her in the near future. Their prospective marriage would be very popular in the neighbourhood. It would go some way to distract attention from the Cobbledick situation, and the publicity would be useful in association with his candidature as prospective M.P. for the constituency. Moreover, even if Jeremy Crabbe landed his Fellowship and he and Amanda announced their engagement, his own marriage in the autumn might be a means of delaying theirs, and even lead to second thoughts. His mind began to debate the most suitable locale for the marriage ceremony. Mallingham Cathedral would be overdoing it a bit, perhaps, as it was, after all, his second marriage. If it had to be at the parish church they could spread themselves over the reception at the Hall. He visualised a large marquee on the lawn . . .

*   *   *

Amanda Railsdon had been half-asleep when she arrived home at half past eleven on the previous night and done little more than stumble upstairs to bed. Her father had taken her for a late dinner to one of the airport hotels. Over the meal and during the drive back to Loxford they had discussed at length his adoption as a parliamentary candidate and the previous day's sensational discoveries in the church, the latter without undue reference to Jeremy Crabbe. Then her father had told her about Pippa Cobbledick's disappearance, startling her into a horrified reaction.

'Of course it's worst of all for the father and mother,'

she said, 'but I hardly know them. It's Bill I'm thinking of. He was crazy about the kid. Always telling you the latest bright thing she'd come out with and whatever.'

However, before long sleep overcame her, and she only woke when the car slowed for the turn into the drive of Loxford House and the gravel crunched familiarly under the wheels.

She awoke to broad daylight and momentarily blinked at the unfamiliar surroundings of her bedroom at home. A glance at the little clock on her bedside table told her that it was half past nine. Her thoughts flew to Jeremy. This was the day – one of the most important in his life and in her own. She lay on her back for a couple of minutes letting a procession of thoughts stream through her mind. Her father and the constituency. Perhaps he would be too busy now to bother about her marrying Jeremy. Was he ever going to propose to Henrietta Legge as everybody expected? Henrietta was definitely pro-Jeremy. Then the incredible events in the parish church the day before yesterday. Surely they would make Jeremy news? Wouldn't he be in the papers today? She leapt out of bed, flung a dressing-gown over her pyjamas and ran downstairs. At the same moment Mrs Bennett emerged from the kitchen, a small, spectacled figure, grey-haired and wearing an immaculate white overall.

'Woken up at last, have you?' she said, enveloped in Amanda's hug. 'You could do with a good breakfast, I'll be bound. Bacon and egg and anything else you fancy. Coffee and rolls don't stay with you, say what you like.'

'D'you know, Benny, I'd adore bacon and eggs and tomatoes. With you, in the kitchen. While you're getting it I'll just have a shower and put something on. Only I just want a quick look at the papers first.'

35

'If it's your young man you're after he's got into the news right enough. Now get along with you. You can read the papers over your breakfast.'

'All right, you bossy old thing,' Amanda called over her shoulder as she ran upstairs two steps at a time. There was genuine affection and confidence between them. During her mother's long terminal illness Mrs Bennett had comforted and reassured in a way that no one else, however well-intentioned, had managed to do.

Upstairs she had a shower and vigorous rub-down, and put on jeans and a flowered cotton top. She had inherited her father's fairness, and as she brushed out her deep gold hair worn in a straight bob she reflected that good stylists were going to be harder to come by in Mallingham or Shirborough than in Paris. Her eyes were grey and her features a small, neat version of her father's, and she had something of his air of intelligence and assurance. Running downstairs she put her head round his study door but the room was empty. Neither was he in the dining-room.

'Benny, where's Daddy?' she asked on arriving in the kitchen.

'I saw him go off in the car half-an-hour ago,' Mrs Bennett replied, putting a laden plate and a teapot in front of her. 'Gone to see Vicar, I expect, about arranging for a rota of stewards down at the church to keep an eye on things for a day or two. Quite a lot of people turned up yesterday afternoon, and we don't want 'em writing their names on the tombs and such-like.'

In the intervals between downing bacon and eggs, Amanda skimmed the various newspapers assembled for her. Under such headings as '*Sensational Treasure Trove in Abbess's Empty Grave*' Mr Jeremy Crabbe, son of the vicar of Loxford, Crantshire, had satisfactory mentions. She looked up to meet Mrs Bennett's interested and enquiring eyes.

'What next, love?' the latter asked.

'You know Daddy's dead against Jeremy and me getting married. He's no use for the sort of career Jeremy's set on. Legally we can marry, of course, but we don't want to start off with a flaming row and bad feeling if it can be helped. So we're waiting to see if Jeremy gets this Research Fellowship at Oxford. You probably know he's there today, having interviews. A job at a university sounds better than teaching in a school, you see!'

'And if he's unlucky?'

Amanda got up and gave her a hug.

'You'll be the first to know, Benny darling . . . How awful of me not to have asked about that poor little grandchild of Bill Cobbledick's.'

'There's no news. Leastways there wasn't on the eight o'clock news this morning.'

'It's simply ghastly,' Amanda said with feeling. 'I think I'll go down to the Vicarage. Bill might have rung . . . So might Jeremy, to be honest.'

Wishing that time would pass more quickly and bring a decision from Oxford one way or the other, she strolled down the drive and made for the village. There were a couple of non-local cars parked outside the church. The south door was ajar, and she peeped in. Two groups of people were wandering around, and an elderly man from the village was seated in a pew, keeping them under observation. There was no sign of her father, so she went on, heading for the Vicarage. As she went up the steps she could hear Erica Crabbe's voice taking part in a telephone conversation. The next moment there came the sound of the receiver being replaced and Erica appeared in the hall.

'Amanda!' she exclaimed warmly. 'How nice to have you home again,' and gave her a hug.

37

'Has Daddy been here?' Amanda asked, after answering queries about her examination papers and the journey home.

'No, my dear. I haven't seen him this morning. That was Martin on the line, ringing from the holiday camp. Of course you've heard all about poor little Pippa Cobbledick vanishing in this terrifying way. Martin drove down there after breakfast to see if he could possibly help over anything. Apparently the police have told the child's parents that they're satisfied that she isn't anywhere locally that she could have got to on her own, and have advised them and Bill to go home. Of course they – the police – will be keeping in touch with the parents. Martin says Bill and Ethel are leaving almost at once, so I simply must dash along and alert their neighbours about getting food in, and so on . . . Come in for a good natter as soon as things are a bit less hectic.'

As they walked into the village together Amanda ventured to ask if Jeremy had rung.

'Not a cheep from him,' Erica replied. 'Before he went he told us not to expect any quick decision about the Fellowship, you know.'

'Well, I think I'll drop in on Henrietta next,' Amanda said. 'Daddy might possibly have gone to see her about something. See you and Martin soon, anyway.'

Henrietta Legge's cottage, built early in the nineteenth century, was at the end of a short cul-de-sac leading off the village street. In spite of the ten years between them she had to some extent filled the place of an elder sister to Amanda, and had been in her confidence over the love affair with Jeremy Crabbe. About an unhappy earlier love affair of her own she had been more reticent. As she walked up the lane, Amanda wondered if Henrietta would be happy if she became Mrs Railsdon. Her father was fun, of course, and certainly generous. Everything in

38

the garden super – unless you crossed him over anything important. There would be quite a lot of public life now, some of it interesting, and plenty of cash. Perceptively, she had observed from various small matters that Henrietta was hard up these days.

As usual she tried the handle of the front door, found it unlocked and walked into the little hall.

'Hen-ri-et-ta,' she called on a rising scale.

'In here,' came in reply, after a momentary pause, from the sitting-room at the front of the cottage which overlooked the garden.

She stopped dead with one foot over the threshold. Her father and Henrietta Legge were sitting side-by-side on the sofa, his arm along its back behind her shoulders. There was a quiet satisfaction and the faintest touch of uncertainty in their greetings. Then a broad grin spread over Basil Railsdon's face.

'Meet your stepmother, Mandy darling,' he invited.

With a quick movement she was across the room and stooping to kiss Henrietta who hugged her affectionately.

'Such an awful word, stepmother,' the latter said. 'It suggests Cinderella and tear-jerking Victorian novels.'

Amanda kissed her father and perched on the arm of the sofa beside him.

'I'm thrilled to bits,' she told them. 'I was wondering if you were ever going to pop the question, Daddy. When is it to be?'

It transpired that they had agreed without hesitation on a special licence and very quiet London wedding, with only the closest relatives and friends invited.

'Then later we'll have a slap-up reception at Loxford House,' her father said. 'Ask all the people we want, and quite a lot of locals we don't, including Party officials, for sheer vulgar publicity. I can visualise Henrietta coping with them to perfection. We thought the wedding itself

in early September, before the constituency winter programme gets going. We're going into Mallingham now to
choose the ring, aren't we, love?'

When Henrietta had gone upstairs to get ready Basil
patted the sofa where she had been sitting. Amanda slipped into the vacant space.

'You don't mind, Mandy, do you?'

'Mind?' she echoed. 'Of course not, Daddy. I'm most
awfully glad. And I'm sure it's what Mummy would have
wanted you to do.'

'Yes,' he said. 'She told me before she went that she
hoped I'd marry again.'

'And as far as I'm concerned it's not as though you're
marrying a stranger who'd look on me as a sort of unwel-
come appendage. And anyway, I may be getting a job, in
London probably – *Highly trained secretary. Fluent
French.* You know. And by the way,' she went on, feeling that this was not the moment to introduce the subject
of her own possible engagement in the near future, 'I
dropped in at the vicarage on my way here. Erica was
just taking a call from Martin. He'd gone down to the
holiday camp to see if there was any possible way he
could help. But the police told the Cobbledicks that
they're quite certain by now that the poor little kid isn't
anywhere that she could have got to under her own
steam, or been raped and thrown into a local ditch, and
they've advised all the relatives to go home. Bill and Mrs
Bill are coming back this morning. Erica was just going
round to tell their neighbours.'

There was a pause. Looking up, Amanda saw that her
father was staring fixedly at the backs of his hands.

'Ghastly business,' he said at last. 'Knowing Bill as one
does, he'll try to keep himself sane by working like hell
. . . Here's Henrietta. Shall we drop you off at the drive
gate? We shall be lunching in Mallingham of course.'

'That'll be fine. I simply must unpack and begin to get myself sorted out,' she replied briskly. The realisation that from now on she would no longer occupy the first place in her father's domestic arrangements was momentarily disconcerting, but this thought was quickly ousted by an urgent desire to be within easy reach of the Loxford House telephone.

*   *   *

Later that morning, Bill and Ethel Cobbledick drove into Loxford. They looked straight ahead, deliberately not seeing people who were about, and their car disappeared round the side of the house into the yard at the back. When they unlocked the back door and went into the kitchen Ethel broke down at the sight of an appetising cold meal laid out at one end of the table and a vase of flowers arranged on the dresser, the work of sympathetic neighbours. Bill put his arm round her shoulders.

'Work's best when everything's black as midnight,' he said, 'so us better eat. Then I'll be gettin' into workin' clothes and goin' round to see what sort of a mess Walt and Tom'll have made of puttin' that bit o' gravestone back.'

Ethel managed to choke back her tears.

'You'm right,' she said. 'There's that pile of ironin' I left only part done.'

They ate without appetite, but the food and some hot tea did them good. Bill got up from the table and went to change into a boiler-suit. It was the lunch hour and he met only a few acquaintances who tactfully gave him gruff greetings and sympathetic half-salutes as they passed. As Ethel washed up there was a tentative knock at the door. She opened it reluctantly to find a lifelong

41

friend carrying a plate covered with a cloth. Unable to speak she invited her in by a gesture. They sat down, and she found relief in further tears and the intermittent pouring out of the story of the last two days.

By nightfall both Bill and Ethel, while continually listening for the telephone bell, had begun to accept dumbly that ordinary life had got to go on. This was driven home by the fact that Pippa no longer occupied the central columns of the *North Crantshire Evening News*, and the continuing search for her was now one of the later items in the area's local news programme on television. Moreover, other matters of intense interest to Loxford were soon to divert interest from the Cobbledick tragedy. After buying the engagement ring, lunching at the best hotel in Mallingham and visiting his solicitor, Basil Railsdon brought his future bride back to Loxford House. He took her straight to Mrs Bennett's little sitting-room. The latter was completely reassured as to her own future by Henrietta's natural tact, and expressed genuine pleasure.

'Why Sir,' she told Basil, 'I won't say that there haven't been quite a few of us that has been hoping for this bit of news.'

Later she was observed heading for the village on her bicycle, and by the next morning the engagement was virtually common knowledge and widely approved. Meanwhile, the coverage given by the press and the media to the discoveries in the church had already started off a steady trickle of visitors who were also eager to explore Loxford itself and make purchases at its shops.

Basil Railsdon slept uneasily that night, waking several times to an awareness of the possible threat to himself of a returned Bill Cobbledick avid for work as an analgesic and taking up the section of the gravestone

42

replaced by Walt White and Tom Moss. After breakfast he returned to his bedroom and focussed a pair of powerful binoculars on the east end of the church and the gravel sweep on the north side. The Cobbledicks' van was parked outside the vestry door but there was no sign of a police car or any other vehicle. He stood assessing the situation. Bill habitually started his working day at eight a.m. It was now nearly half past nine, and there was no sign of Walt White's battered Austin or Tom Moss's motorbike, so apparently they had not been summoned to help shift the section of the gravestone which they had replaced on their own. It was a reasonable assumption that Bill was working alone, fixing the second piece in position and filling in the crack with mortar. Basil decided to go down to the church. It was, he told himself, his last fence.

His reasoning had been perfectly correct. Bill Cobbledick was on his knees by the grave, and the scrape of a trowel on stone greeted Basil's ears as he came through the vestry.

Bill looked up without speaking, his face drawn and set.

'I'm not going to talk, Bill,' Basil said. 'You know well enough what we're all feeling. But I saw your van and couldn't just walk past.'

Bill nodded, and went on skilfully filling in the crack between the two pieces of the gravestone. Basil went out quietly, conscious of a sense of profound relief. Fatal road accidents happen every day, he thought. They'll get over it. Much better for the kid than being crippled by injuries.

Chapter Three

Jeremy Crabbe rang at midday. Amanda, tense with long expectation, gave the Loxford House number in what she hoped was a normal voice.

'Home and dry,' he said, also trying to convey adult impassivity. Then, on hearing her gasp of delight he abandoned the attempt. 'Mandy, it's – well, it means –' he told her, 'scope, facilities, the lot, and marrying you, now that I've got a toe-hold on the academic ladder. You haven't changed your mind, have you?'

'I'd have expected a Fellow of Athanasius to have a better grasp of fundamentals. When are you getting back?'

'Unfortunately they've asked me to stay to lunch. I'll escape as soon as I decently can and drive straight down, even if it's only for an hour. I ought to make it by about five. Meet at the vicarage, don't you think?'

'Yes, I do. Getting Daddy to accept the situation may take more than an hour.'

'Too true, I'm afraid. Well darling, see you.'

'Jeremy, hang on for one more minute. Something important's happened. Daddy's proposed to Henrietta at long last, and the wedding's to be in September. It'll be in *The Times* tomorrow. I'm terribly glad for her, and anyway it will take his mind off us.'

Jeremy whistled. 'Things,' he said, 'do seem to be going for us at the moment, don't they? Now I'll ring the parents. Bless you, my darling love. See you in a few hours.'

Amanda put down the receiver and plunged into the kitchen to brief Mrs Bennett.

While comparatively few of the inhabitants of Loxford were clear about what a Junior Research Fellowship at Athanasius College, Oxford, was, it was generally agreed that young Jeremy Crabbe had come out on top again in some way. The crowded Saturday night bar of the Ring of Bells was full of this new item of local news, and there were forecasts of another engagement in the Railsdon family before long. The Cobbledick tragedy receded yet a little further from the centre of the stage.

To Amanda's satisfaction her father was due to attend the annual dinner of a Shirborough society of which he was Vice-President. She invited herself to supper with Henrietta, and hurried to Abbey Cottage as soon as Jeremy had driven off from the vicarage to resume his present job at Mallingham College. Radiant, she poured out his reactions to his prospects at Athanasius and their plans to marry at the end of the autumn term.

'Even if Daddy's simply bloody about it and just contracts out, we're going ahead,' she told Henrietta, 'but I'm sure you can help calm him down. Jeremy's coming over after tea tomorrow, and we're breaking it to Daddy then.'

'Actually I'm coming up to tea with Basil. He wants to show me over the house with an eye to future arrangements. I don't know if you think it would be a help or not for me to be around?'

Amanda considered. 'Well, if it was an ordinary

situation – I mean a daughter bringing along a perfectly eligible fiancé to show her father – surely she'd want her future stepmother to be in on it, too, especially if she happened to be fond of her? I mean, there's something to be said for assuming people are going to behave normally and sensibly, don't you think?'

'A good question, as T.V. interviewers comment so patronisingly. Yes, I agree. I'll do my best to say the right thing at the right moment.'

'Bless you. The fact that you're marrying Daddy helps enormously.'

As they talked, it struck Amanda that Henrietta seemed more relaxed and happy than she had been for some time. She wondered shrewdly whether she loved her future husband, or whether the prospect of financial security was a great relief. She was not to know until some time afterwards that one of Basil's first steps had been to pay off the mortgage Henrietta had raised on Abbey Cottage, and arrange for the new unencumbered deeds to be returned to her.

*　　　*　　　*

Nearly twenty-four hours later Jeremy and Amanda walked hand-in-hand into Basil Railsdon's study, where he was having a late tea with Henrietta. There was a surprised silence followed by Basil's congratulations on the Fellowship, in which she joined.

'Thanks very much,' Jeremy said. 'Of course I'm pretty bucked about it myself. Quite apart from what it's going to mean for my research, I feel justified now in asking Mandy to marry me. I'm happy to say she's accepted me.'

There was a longer and decidedly tense silence before Basil spoke.

46

'In my opinion Amanda is too young and too socially inexperienced to rush into this marriage. She has been abroad most of the time since she left school, and hasn't had the opportunity of moving in the extensive circle of my friends and acquaintances, which includes people who are outstanding in various spheres of public life. If I could legally forbid the marriage I should do so.'

Amanda, who had subsided into an armchair, eyed him critically.

'What I can't understand is,' she said, 'why, if you're so dead set on bringing outstanding figures in public life into the family, you haven't gone for somebody with a title or an O.B.E. or something instead of Henrietta.'

Henrietta herself was the first to dissolve into helpless laughter, followed by Amanda and Jeremy. In spite of all his efforts the corners of Basil's mouth twitched.

'You're an absolute little bitch, Mandy,' he told her. 'Always have been. Spoilt from the cradle. Well, go your own way. You'll fetch up in the divorce court in a few years when you've realised what you're throwing away, but broken marriages are the order of the day, I suppose. Might I ask when and where you're proposing to marry?'

'December the sixteenth,' Jeremy replied, 'the day after term ends at Mallingham School. As to where, well, we haven't got as far as that. I suppose my father will want to marry us. We haven't told the parents it's definitely fixed up yet: I thought I should come to you first.'

'Of course Mandy must be married from her own home,' Henrietta came in. 'I shall simply adore organising everything.'

47

'Nothing lush,' Amanda said hurriedly. 'Not our line, is it Jeremy?'

'We'd like it to be just family and our own inner circle,' he agreed.

Basil Railsdon took out a pocket-book and a gold propelling-pencil.

'What's your full name?' he asked.

'Jeremy Hamlyn Crabbe. Hamlyn with a y.'

'The engagement should be in *The Times* by Wednesday,' Basil commented, reaching for the day's issue of the paper. 'As I've said, I don't approve of the marriage. However, you're both legally entitled to go through with it. But please take it as read that I'm not standing for my daughter's marriage being a hole-and-corner affair . . . And now, Henrietta and I have various affairs of our own to discuss.'

'We'll fade out then,' Amanda replied, levering herself out of her armchair. 'Come on, Jeremy.'

Jeremy bade Basil and Henrietta a polite good evening and followed her out of the room.

'Not a drop of bubbly,' she commented as they emerged from the house. 'I always thought something of the sort was *de rigueur* on these occasions. Still, Daddy could have been a lot worse . . . Jeremy, can you really believe we're going to be married?'

'With difficulty.' Glancing round, he embraced her passionately behind a clump of rhododendrons.

'Does this place mean an awful lot to you?' he asked, looking at Loxford House over her shoulder.

'Not really, although it's always been my home. Interesting architecturally, of course, and quite good to look at, but it lacks something – I don't quite know what. Anyway, we shall never fetch up there. Henrietta will have sons. That's part of the idea, I'm sure.'

'To Henrietta and Basil Railsdon M.P., a son,'

Jeremy said thoughtfully. 'What's happening over there?' He indicated a stack of building materials by the feedstore.

'Daddy's having the garages in the old stable block repaired and re-roofed. Bill Cobbledick's been doing it, so I expect there'll be a bit of a hold-up, although he's working quite madly from all accounts. Still no news of Pippa, I suppose?'

'None. Dad says he doesn't believe the police have got a single lead.'

They turned and walked down the drive and through the village to the vicarage, still hand-in-hand and oblivious of surreptitiously parted curtains. By nightfall the news of their engagement was the chief topic of conversation in Loxford.

Basil Railsdon, as chairman of several companies and an executive member of the boards of several others, had evolved a number of techniques for handling people in dicey situations. On the following day he went to see Martin and Erica Crabbe, and began by being disarmingly frank.

'Of course you'll have gathered that I should have liked the marriage at any rate postponed,' he said. 'I don't feel that Mandy has met enough men and moved in a wide enough circle to make a decision at this juncture. But I do want you to believe that I like Jeremy and respect his undoubted ability. I think he is set fair for a distinguished academic career. And let's face it, the Crabbe family has been gentry-born for generations, and my great-grandfather started off in shirt-sleeves and merely piled up a fortune. Although of course money doesn't come into it. Mandy inherits her mother's money this year. The trustees have handled the capital very competently in consultation with myself, and the final sum won't be less than forty

49

thousand. And she will, of course, eventually have a share in my own estate.'

Martin and Erica Crabbe sat speechless.

'But what on earth will they do with all that money?' Martin asked at last. 'Quite apart from anything Jeremy earns?'

Basil smiled indulgently. 'School fees are rising faster than the current rate of inflation,' he said. 'Perhaps we can all three look forward to the patter of little feet in due course. Now there's one other thing I want to talk to you about. It's highly confidential at the present stage, by the way. Only Henrietta knows about it. My wedding present to Jeremy and Mandy. I'm giving them Abbey Cottage.'

'*Abbey Cottage*?' Erica exclaimed incredulously.

'Yes. It sounds surprising, but let me explain. The idea hit me when Henrietta and I were discussing future plans, and she said it seemed a pity to let it go altogether as it's virtually on Loxford House land. Was there any way of letting it so that we would be sure of being able to regain possession if we ever wanted to? To cut a long story short, we're having it professionally valued, and I am buying it from her and having the deeds transferred to Mandy. It will give her and Jeremy a combination of holiday home and permanent base, and we shall see a lot more of them and any offspring they produce. Good scheme, don't you think?'

Later, after seeing him off from the steps, the Crabbes turned and went back into the house.

'I hope we managed to sound decently appreciative,' Martin said. 'Do you think Abbey Cottage will be the last straw for Jeremy after having had to swallow that forty thousand?'

Erica agreed that it all felt a bit excessive.

'But it can work,' she said. 'The wife having the

50

money, I mean, even on this scale. And Amanda's perceptive as well as intelligent. What riled me was the feeling of being subjected – well – not to a hard sell but a highly experienced one. However, it's time I went to fix the fish pie for supper if we're going to view Jeremy being interviewed on the box.'

*   *   *

As the days passed, life in Loxford reverted increasingly to a more normal course. Local events such as the forthcoming Annual Flower Show began to make their usual demands on people's time and energy. The initial rush of sensationmongers to inspect Aretê Overton's alleged grave became a trickle. The Cobbledicks slowly re-established normal social contacts, although Bill continued to find his main solace in relentless work.

'Bill's starting on re-roofing tomorrow,' Basil Railsdon told Amanda. 'I'm going to move the Hyperion out *pro tem*. There's bound to be a lot of dust. I thought I'd keep it in the old feedstore temporarily.'

'I'll leave mine out round at the back,' she replied. 'It's seen better days and I'll be getting something bigger, of course . . . There's the mail van.'

Basil's mail was increasing steadily as a result of his adoption as prospective Conservative candidate for the area, and of his own and Amanda's forthcoming marriage. He bore off a pile of correspondence to his study, wondering whether it would be worthwhile to get some additional secretarial help at his own expense. It was a temptation to throw anything looking like a circular straight into the waste-paper basket, but he had already learnt to resist it. Some of his potential political supporters were already sending him bunches of newspaper cuttings and lengthy screeds about their hobby horses in large envelopes. As he slit one of these open a birth certificate and a letter fell out. Why the hell, he thought irritably as he picked up the letter, can't constituents go on sending their problems to Conibeer? Damn it, he's still the North Crantshire Member . . .

To his astonishment it began 'Dear Basil'. It was written on vivid blue writing-paper dated two days earlier, and with an address in the London outer suburb of Medstone. The handwriting was small and featureless.

'I am calling you Basil instead of Mr Railsdon, although we have never met,' the writer went on, *'because you are my half-brother. My mother's name is on the birth certificate but no father's name because I am illegitimate. You will also see a copy of an undertaking signed by my mother never to tell me or anybody who my father was, in return for £2,000. He was Charles Basil Railsdon of Loxford. Perhaps you found the original paper my mother signed after our father's death as I did her copy last winter when she died. Then I saw in the paper that a Basil Railsdon of Loxford was going to stand for Parliament and thought I would like to contact you as I have no other relatives living. I work in a big local store here. Yours sincerely, Laura Raymond'*

Basil read the letter twice, formulating the action he would take while doing so. The birth certificate gave the date of Laura Raymond's birth as April 28th 1936. That made her four years older than himself. His parents had married in 1939 just before the War broke out, and he was their eldest and only surviving child. Laura's mother was given as Margaret Raymond, occupation florist. He had a sudden mental vision of his father as a wealthy young man going into a West End florist's and being confronted by an attractive piece in an enchanting floral setting . . . To be fair, not just a piece: Margaret Raymond had stood by the agreement she had signed. The old man had behaved decently, too. £2,000 was quite a tidy sum in 1936.

Reaching for a sheet of Loxford House writing-paper Basil wrote to the partner in a London firm of solicitors who dealt with Railsdon family business. The first step was verification, of course. The whole thing could be a try-on, but there was a feel of authenticity about it somehow. The woman was after money, no doubt. If she had lived with her mother the latter's retirement pension would have stopped. Make her an allowance, perhaps, but on no account get personally involved, he thought, putting his own letter and Laura Raymond's with its two enclosures into an envelope. As he did so he decided to keep the whole matter to himself, at any rate for the present. Perhaps he would tell Henrietta after they were married.

Miles Walker, the solicitor to whom he had written, was a contemporary and had become a personal friend over the years. His reply came ten days later. After making a few amused comments he stated categorically that beyond any doubt Laura Raymond actually was the illegitimate daughter of Basil's father, and that the writer of the letter was indisputably Laura Raymond and none other. The birth certificate was genuine, and discreet enquiries had established that she had lived with her mother, believed to be a war widow, in Medstone from her later childhood, had gone to the local secondary modern school, and was now employed in a local store. The mother had died. In response to Miles Walker's request Laura had come to see him at his office on her half-day, which was Wednesday.

'*As you will have deduced from her letter,*' Miles Walker wrote, '*She is certainly not of your education and social class. On the other hand there is nothing objectionable or loud about her. She is rather quiet, dresses*

53

for her age, sparing of make-up. If anything, slightly drab. She told me that her mother had left her a little money and the Medstone semi, and that she herself was earning quite a good salary and hoped to keep on their small car, but I did not get any impression that she thought you might be a soft touch. But I agree that a modest allowance from you would be an appropriate gesture. It could be handled by us if you like, to avoid any personal involvement. It seemed to me that she is getting a kick out of discovering that she has a half-brother living at a classy address and likely to become an M.P. before long, and hopes for a closer acquaintance. It would not have struck me if I had just met her out of the blue, but there is a slight "Railsdon" look about her – in the shape of her nose, mouth and chin . . .'

Basil Railsdon read his solicitor's letter with interest, and sat at his desk considering the alternative courses of action open to him. Should he communicate with Laura Raymond solely through Henshaw, Walker and Henshaw, and have an annual allowance – of, say £200 – paid to her through them? Or should he after all answer her letter personally, and propose a meeting in London at which he would show a sympathetic attitude towards her history and make the offer of the allowance?

He was invariably concerned with the image he pre-sented in his different spheres. As the owner of Loxford House, on the one hand, as a leading figure in the affairs of the village and its neighbourhood, and as the adopted candidate of the Conservative party in the North Crantshire constituency. He now had to choose between the two potential images that he could present to Laura Raymond: a busy man prepared to accept a measure of financial responsibility, but not for any personal involvement, or a surprised but kindly kinsman, ready to make her an allowance and to keep in occasional touch to assure himself that all was well with her.

Eventually he came down on the side of the second image. It passed through his mind that it could be incorporated into the one he reserved for his intimate friends – 'As a matter of fact, old boy, a bastard half-sister's suddenly come to light. Father was a bit of a rip in his younger days, you know . . . Oh, no, I haven't got to fork out in a big way. She's forty-six and in a job, and has a small house in suburbia. Father paid up. But I felt that in common decency I should make her a modest allowance . . .'

Something like that. Quite casual, but conveying the sort of impression one would like to make. He began to draft a letter in reply to Laura Raymond's.

Their relationship, he told her, was a complete surprise to him. He felt sure that she would understand that he had felt obliged to have the facts she gave him verified by his solicitor. This had now been done to his own complete satisfaction, and the next step must be a personal meeting to which he was looking forward with interest. He understood from Mr Walker that she was free on Wednesday afternoons. Would she care to have tea with him at the Britannia Hotel close to Victoria Station on either of the two following Wednesdays, at four p.m.? He assumed that she would be coming up from Medstone by train.

After finishing off the letter he put it with the rest of his outgoing mail and strolled out into the garden for a breath of air, feeling satisfied with the proposed programme. He had to offer her a meal, of course, and tea was less formal than lunch and less intimate than dinner, as well as being less time-consuming than either. And the Britannia, good class without being pretentious, an eminently suitable place for the meeting.

Intermittent small crashes and thuds were coming from

55

behind the house. He went round to the old stables to find Bill Cobbledick up a ladder, dislodging slates and throwing them down to his nephew Walt White below who was loading them into a trailer. On seeing Basil approaching Bill descended.

'Mornin', Sir,' he said. 'I reckon one or two of the rafters needs renewin' as well as the battens.'

'Right,' Basil told him. 'Make a thorough job of it Bill, while you're about it. It's going to look fine. I managed to get genuine old pantiles in good condition from a firm doing a demolition job. They're stacked at the back of the feedstore. Move the car out if it's difficult to get at them. And what's more, I've picked up an old weathercock. I've always wanted one, and this is the obvious place for it. I brought it back yesterday and it's down in the feedstore too. Go and have a look at it and see what you think is the best way of rigging it up here.'

Bill Cobbledick became conversational to the point of saying he'd often fancied a weathercock himself. After further chat Basil went off to get his car and drop in on Henrietta, reflecting that Bill was more like his old self.

Her engagement had brought a new confidence and buoyancy to Henrietta. She looked charming, Basil thought, as she came running down the stairs to greet him on hearing his car. As they sat over elevenses, talking about future plans, it was borne in on him that it was going to be pleasant to have her there to discuss day-to-day problems with, and that he was more anxious than he had realised to stand well in her eyes. What would be her reaction, he wondered, to the Laura Raymond situation.

*   *   *

56

On the Wednesday of his fixture with Laura Raymond, Basil Railsdon was at pains to arrive at the Britannia Hotel in good time. He booked a table for tea in the lounge and seated himself in the reception area with a good view of the main entrance. She arrived on the stroke of four. He identified her without hesitation and went forward with a welcoming smile and outstretched hand.

'Laura?' he said interrogatively.

'That's right.' She shook hands rather clumsily.

'Come along to the lounge and we'll have some tea. I've booked a table.'

As he shepherded her they exchanged a few disjointed remarks of a general character and he registered his first impressions. He had been prepared by Miles Walker for a non-U voice and unsmart clothes, but had not expected quite such gauche unresponsiveness. Still, he reflected, it was understandable enough that she should have a chip on the shoulder. Miles had been right about her Railsdon mouth and chin, but the family resemblance ended there. She was short, with light brown hair and brown eyes.

Over tea he extracted a bald outline of her previous history. She had no clear memory of it herself, but her mother had told her that her earliest years had been spent in a small terrace house in Brixton. They had been evacuated to Wales in 1939, and their house was destroyed in the blitz. A house in Medstone had been bought with the war damage money. She had gone to the local schools, and when her maintenance allowance, paid through a solicitor, had stopped at her sixteenth birthday she had got her first job as a junior shop assistant. From this she had moved on to other local jobs and ended up in her present one as stock manager in a big store.

'This is a story which does great credit to both your mother and yourself,' Basil said, after a suitable pause. 'What I'm anxious to do now is to make life a bit easier for you. I propose making you an allowance of two hundred pounds a year. Index-linked, of course,' he added, smiling at her.

As their eyes met he was puzzled by the expression in hers. Was it just satisfaction at his offer or something more? One could almost detect a gleam of triumph.

'It's not your money I'm after,' she said, with an emphasis on the word money.

'Well, Laura, I'd be only too glad to help you out financially if you'd let me, but if you don't want it, what can I do for you?'

She abruptly planted her elbows on the table and stared at him aggressively.

'Stands out a mile, I'd've thought. Forty-six years I've been under the carpet. Time I came out and was taken for who I am. Half my blood's the same as half yours, for all you're such a big pot down at Loxford. Oh, yes, I've been down to Loxford and seen your great posh house from the outside. After my Mum died and I found that paper saying who my Dad was I went to the Library, and they gave me a book called *Who's Who* for looking up big bugs.'

On the horizon of Basil Railsdon's mind an appalling possibility suddenly presented itself, but it was so remote and improbable that he dismissed it and concentrated on cooling the atmosphere.

'But why on earth didn't you write and tell me that you were coming down to Loxford?' he asked.

'Lucky for me I didn't, the way things turned out,' she replied. The gloating note in her voice was unmistakeable, and Basil felt himself gripped by cold apprehension. 'I decided I'd like a look round first, see?'

Her employers had been sympathetic over her mother's death, and ready to give her an extra week's holiday at Easter. She had driven down to Shirborough, put up at a small hotel, and the next day driven over to Loxford. It had, however, been an abortive trip. During a visit to the Post Office, ostensibly to buy some picture postcards, she had chatted and learnt that Mr Railsdon of Loxford House was away and not expected back until the evening, and that next day he was being adopted as the future Conservative parliamentary candidate for North Crantshire. There was to be a meeting in Shirborough. It would be quite something for Loxford people, she had been told, having the M.P. living in the village. He'd get in, sure enough. It was a safe Tory seat. Old Mr Conibeer'd had a majority of nearly twenty thousand last time.

Returning to Shirborough, she had explored the area around the Conservative Association's office, and found a useful car park just opposite. The next morning she arrived there an hour before the Adoption Meeting was due to start, and parked close to the exit. A small crowd gathered on the pavement and Basil's arrival in his gleaming white Hyperion was greeted by cheers and shouts of 'Up Railsdon' from his supporters. Waving to them, he had hurried across the road and gone into the Conservative office. She had sat waiting in the car until at long last he came out again.

'Then you stood on the steps talking to some old buffer for God knows how long,' Laura went on, her accent thickening and her voice rising, 'but I'd got it all lined up. I banked on your going home, and with any luck having some of your classy friends in to celebrate. Just the moment for me to walk in. I started up the engine and came out of the car park on your tail. I knew I couldn't keep up with a car like yours, but I had

59

luck at some road repairs where you were held up, and just saw you turn off down that lane and followed on.' Her eyes glinted. 'So I saw it all,' she ended triumphantly.

As she talked, Basil managed to control his rising panic and rapidly considered the options open to him.

'Saw what?' he asked in a tone of incomprehension.

'You needn't try that line on me,' Laura retorted. 'It won't wash. I'd just come up to the top of a hill when I saw your car stopped at the bottom on the wrong side, and some bloody funny business going on. I let mine run back out of your sight, and got out and watched from close up to the hedge. Your boot was open and you were putting something into it. I could see a small kid's legs dangling all limp. You locked the boot and went to the front of the car and had a good look round. Then you got in and drove off. It was clear as daylight thát you'd killed the kid. You don't put injured people in car boots to take 'em to hospital. It looked as though I'd been dealt the ace of trumps. When the news of the little girl gone missing came on the radio that evening I went to the Shirborough police station, and told 'em I'd been on the coast road as they call it between the times they said, being on holiday and thinking I might get a good view of the coast, but hadn't seen any other car on it. I realised,' she concluded, with an exceedingly unpleasant smile, 'that it could pay me better to keep my trap shut, see? It meant waiting to see if they'd find the body, but I reckon you've been too smart for them. So what?'

By dint of exercising almost superhuman control Basil managed to keep his head.

'My dear Laura,' he said, 'You've been reading too many whodunits or watching too many crime films on

60

the box! Really, I can hardly help laughing! I certainly did stop at the bottom of a hill on the coast road and open the boot because there was a certain amount of junk in it that was rattling about and getting on my nerves. I can only imagine that your dangling legs were a coil of rope for cordoning off a bit of the lawn that needs treatment. And I admit going round to the front of the car to have a look at my offside tyre which I thought could be a bit down.'

He watched a momentary hesitation in her face and immediately drove home his advantage.

'You've had a trying time, both over your mother's death and all your life, come to that,' he went on in a different key, 'and I don't wonder that it's made you feel that no holds are barred. But let's get back to what you were saying you wanted me to do: accept you as a member of what we'll call the Loxford part of the family. I was just going to suggest that you might like to come down to Loxford House when you have your summer holiday, and stay with my daughter and myself, and meet Henrietta Legge who is becoming my second wife early in September. But late July or August would be all right, especially the first part.'

There was a long silence which he found almost intolerable.

'I don't think I believe you,' she said at last. 'I'd rather believe my own eyes. But if you did kill that kid and somehow got rid of the body for good, well, that's that. If you went to jail I wouldn't get what I'm out for, would I?. My holiday's the first two weeks in August.'

'Well, that fits in very well, doesn't it?' Basil said. 'When I get home, I'll have a look at my diary and write to you to fix dates.'

She shot an astute glance at him.

'What I'd like would be to move down to your part of

the world for keeps. Get a job there. Shirborough's quite a big town with some big stores. I took a look round when I was there . . . Maybe you own some nice little cottages in Loxford. . . .'

Chapter Four

Jeremy Crabbe's coup over Aretê Overton's alleged grave in Loxford church was undoubtedly a factor in his election to the Junior Research Fellowship at Oxford. It also brought him some acceptable spin-offs. These included his television interview, and some requests for contributions from various newspapers and journals. He was also approached by a leading publishing house about writing a book which would deal with the discovery in more detail and in its historical context. As soon as his summer term at Mallingham College was over he went up to London to discuss the proposition with the editor concerned.

'Well, darling,' he told Amanda on his return, 'it's in the bag. Or to put it another way, I've let myself in for it. It's to be called *The Overton Enigma*, and they'd like it by next Easter. I've been getting cold feet on the way back. There's the hell of a lot of work involved. If possible I'd like to rustle up a bit more about the Overtons and Aretê herself, and then there's the historical context as they put it. I'm not all that genned up on the Dissolution, let alone Byzantine goldsmithery. Then there's next term plus the Oxbridge candidates, not to mention our wedding day the moment it's over . . .

Darling, *you* aren't getting cold feet, are you? In my anxious moments I hear a still, small voice saying, "Oh, well, we hardly ever go out, you know. My husband's so immersed in his work." . . .'

'Tell it to shut up,' Amanda replied. 'I foresaw all this from the moment I realised we were falling for each other, and thought it all out. One has to take the job with the chap. I'm positive that quite a lot of marriages go on the rocks because women don't grasp this simple fact. Or men either, come to that, if they marry career women. Incidentally, you won't mind if I land a part-time job in Oxford, I take it, while you research at Athanasius, since we've decided not to start our family right away?'

They had climbed up to the crest of the downland ridge behind Loxford House, and were lying on the turf. Jeremy buried his face in her hair, remarking in a muffled voice that absolutely nothing in the world mattered as long as she didn't regret saying she'd marry him.

'What bit of this programme are you going to start on?' she asked him presently.

'I think I'd better go north the day after tomorrow, and see if I can unearth anything more about Aretê's doings there. Not to Hollowdale – at least not to start with. But it's just remotely possible that she made a Will, and that it's survived in the County Archives at Wellham.'

'She must have had a certain amount of cash to get herself from one end of England to the other, mustn't she?'

'This is it. And if she lived in a very humble way at Hollowdale she might have had a spot to leave. To the church, probably.'

This plan was duly carried out. Amanda had a call

64

from Jeremy in the evening of his day at Wellham. He had started from Loxford at first light and arrived in time to look in on the County Archives Department before it closed. He reported it well-found with helpful staff, and that he was going through the mid-sixteenth century Wills the next day. Twenty-four hours later he rang her again in jubilant mood.

'My hunch about Aretê having made a Will has paid off,' he told her. 'The archives here have a super collection of Wills and were able to track down hers quite quickly. It was made in 1541. She left somebody called Joan Woodman her chattels and ten marks – quite a nice little sum in those days. The originals of the Hollowdale parish registers are here, and we pressed on to see if we could find out anything about this Joan Woodman. Her burial at Hollowdale was in 1555, and she's recorded as aged 57 and widow of this parish. Then we worked backwards to see if her marriage or her husband's death were in the register, but drew a blank. Not surprising really, as a register wasn't kept before 1539. So we knocked off for the day . . . I'm putting up at a very decent little pub here.'

The following evening Amanda got another equally triumphant call. A Thomas Woodman made a Will in 1538, leaving his cottage in Hollowdale, the meadow belonging to it, and the household goods to his wife Joan.

'It looks as though he made it when he knew he was going to pass on, as his death doesn't appear in the register,' Jeremy said. 'The Woodmans were obviously a Hollowdale family. We came across a lot of their baptisms and marriages and burials yesterday. I'm going on to Hollowdale tomorrow in the chance of picking up something more about Joan. I'd like to discover her maiden name if I could.'

This visit, however, was unproductive in spite of active help from the vicar whom Jeremy had met when he had called in at Hollowdale before with such momentous results. There were no longer any Woodmans living in the village, and even the oldest inhabitants could not remember a family of that name. Reporting to Amanda, Jeremy announced his intention of driving back in the course of the night.

'Terrific,' she said. 'I'll ring the vicarage and tell them to leave the catch up. Daddy's getting back some time tonight. Roll on tomorrow, I'm sick of answering letters congratulating me on our engagement, and helping Henrietta sort out her possessions.

*　　　*　　　*

An early telephone call from Erica Crabbe on the following morning informed her that Jeremy had turned up, raided the larder and retired to bed where he was now dead to the world.

'Come down for some elevenses,' she said. 'He'll have surfaced by then.'

On arriving at the Vicarage Amanda found her future husband devouring bacon and eggs at the kitchen table, tousle-headed and in an ancient dressing-gown.

'I realise I'm not looking my best,' he said after leaping up and hugging her, 'but it's just as well for you to know the worst before we're married. I had a super run down and the trip's been well worth it. I got more than I'd hoped for. My guess is that Aretê boarded with the Woodmans, and was looked after by Joan during her last years. Hence the legacy and the chattels. Absence of proof isn't conclusive proof, of course, but there isn't the slightest hint of either Joan or Thomas Woodman having any connection with the Overtons or Loxford Abbey.'

66

After a few minutes' chat Erica left them. Jeremy shot a glance at Amanda.

'I can see you're bursting with news,' he said. 'What's on offer?'

'Well, Daddy came in about half-past nine last night looking a bit jaded. Benny had put out drinks in his study as usual, and he poured himself out a stiffish whisky, slumped into his chair and announced that he'd learnt for the first time that he'd got an illegitimate sister, about four years older than he is. He'd just broken the news to Henrietta over dinner.'

'Worse troubles at sea I should have thought,' Jeremy commented. 'How come he'd known nothing about it up to now?'

'Grandpa – supported by Great Grandpa, I should think – went to enormous lengths to hush it up. The mother seems to have worked in a florist's in the West End. A maintenance allowance was arranged through a firm of solicitors and the mother was offered a down payment of a couple of thousand for signing a statement in which she swore never to let the child or anybody else know who the father was. And she kept her word. She must have been a decent sort.'

'Very decent. I'm sure that sort of statement wouldn't be legally binding. How has it all come out now?'

'The mother died recently, and the daughter found the statement when she went through some papers. She's by no means a fool, Daddy says, and looked him up in *Who's Who*. She came down and stayed in Shirborough over the Easter weekend, came over and vetted Loxford House from the outside, and decided to make herself known. She wrote to Daddy and sent him her birth certificate and a copy of the statement her mother signed. He got them investigated by his London

67

solicitor, and apparently they're perfectly genuine, so he went up to London and met her. He offered her an allowance, but she said she didn't want money specially, but to be accepted by the family.'

'And I suppose she's patently non-U and in his eyes there's a major social problem ahead?'

'That's right. She works in a store in Medstone. In the end, Daddy says, he felt there was nothing for it but to invite her to stay for a week of her annual holiday.'

'When's that?'

'The first two weeks in August. And Daddy wants us both to be at tea this afternoon – Henrietta's coming too – and decide which is the easier week, and how to cope generally. He says Henrietta is being marvellous about it.'

'O.K. by me, anyway,' Jeremy replied. 'Quite honestly I can't see that there's all that much to cope with. Except for the stickiest county circles I should think people will feel it's rather a joke. Now about our plans for the next few weeks . . .'

On arriving home for lunch Amanda learnt from Mrs Bennett that her father had gone over to Miss Legge's for a bite, but that they'd both be back to tea.

'Jeremy's coming along too,' Amanda told her.

'That's right,' Mrs Bennett replied with satisfaction. 'A nice little family party. I'll knock up a plate of my scones.'

When the tea party had assembled Amanda noticed that her father had recovered his usual buoyancy. The explanation was simple enough. Henrietta was adapting herself to her new role with surprising speed and effortlessness. He's beginning to turn to her, she thought. It's the feeling that there's somebody there to turn to. She felt a pang of compunction at not having realised more fully the gap in his life her mother's death must have left, in spite of the long illness leading up to it. His attitude to Jeremy seemed to have changed for the better, too. It was friendly, and there was interest in the discoveries made in the Wellham archives.

After a discussion it was agreed to invite Laura Raymond down for the first week in August, leaving the rest of the month clear for the preparations for Henrietta and Basil's wedding.

'It's not going to be easy, let's face it,' Basil said. 'Laura doesn't speak our language – literally or metaphorically – and I'm afraid she's bound to feel a fish out of water. We must just do what we can. Take her around and get in the sort of people to meet her who'll know how to react. I'll write to her tonight. She hasn't a phone . . . Well, now, there's something else Henrietta and I want to talk to you two about,' he went on. Our wedding present to you. We've decided to make it a joint one. We're giving you Abbey Cottage. It can be your base over the next three years while Jeremy's holding his Fellowship, and a holiday cottage when he gets something more permanent.'

There was a staggered silence.

'This is how we're arranging things,' Basil went on. 'We're having it professionally valued – a chap from Ling and Tucker of Mallingham is coming over. I shall then buy it from Henrietta retaining part of the purchase price as her contribution, so that it's our joint present, as I said just now. And we're having the deeds transferred to Amanda.'

'But Henrietta,' Amanda gasped, 'you simply *love* Abbey Cottage! How can you bear to part with it? I mean, you could let it. Partly furnished, or whatever a landlord has to do to be able to give a tenant notice.'

'If Basil beats me and I decide to leave him, Mandy darling, I'd hardly want to live on his doorstep, would I?' Henrietta asked.

69

'Mandy's probably anticipating my demise,' Basil said with a grin. 'Thinking of it as a Dower House, and a half-brother in possession here.'

Before Amanda could protest Jeremy cut in.

'I'm pretty speechless,' he said. 'It's such a – well, inspired and magnificent gift that I can't think of anything adequate to say. I feel it's like King Cophetua and the beggarmaid in reverse.'

'No need to see things in that light,' Basil replied. 'Abbey Cottage is a small affair compared with what you two will give Henrietta and me if your marriage turns out well, and I'm coming round to thinking it's got a fifty-fifty chance of that . . .'

'God bless Henrietta,' Amanda remarked as she and Jeremy made their way to the vicarage to break the news to his parents. 'She's brought him round, of course.'

'Don't deduce from that that *you're* going to be able to twist *me* round your little finger, my girl,' Jeremy told her.

'You wait.' She stopped suddenly. 'Look, there it is. Abbey Cottage. Roughly equidistant from both sets of parents, and near but not too near.'

Jeremy squeezed her arm and agreed. At the same time a slightly puzzled look came into his eyes.

*　　*　　*

In reply to Basil Railsdon's letter Laura Raymond accepted his invitation and his offer to meet her train at Shirborough.

'I told her I couldn't offer her a garage for her car because of the re-roofing,' he said to his daughter. 'Bill Cobbledick's behind schedule because of so much of the woodwork having to be renewed. I'm damned if

70

I'm going to have a practically brand new Hyperion outside in all weathers. What room are you putting her in?'

'The one next to mine. It's jolly nice on that side. Morning sun and a gorgeous view.'

'I hope to God we can persuade her to have breakfast in bed. Make sure there's a comfortable chair in the room, and some books if you can find anything suitable. Magazines – the sort most women seem to read – might be better. Her train gets to Shirborough at three-forty-seven next Tuesday, August the third, she says.'

'That's a nuisance. I wish she was coming on Monday. I've got a hair appointment in Mallingham on Wednesday morning. Would you rather I changed it?' Amanda asked.

'No, don't bother,' Basil said, consulting his diary. 'I'm free on Wednesday morning and can take her out for a drive or whatever. You can cope in the afternoon. It might be a good idea to ask the Crabbes or one or two other locals to tea on Wednesday.'

Tuesday was sunny and warm. Shortly before three Basil brought the Hyperion round to the front door of Loxford House. Amanda gave a final glance at the room prepared for Laura Raymond, and came downstairs and slipped into the passenger seat beside her father. They turned right on coming out of the drive gates and headed for Shirborough.

'How do you suppose she'll react to the set-up here?' Amanda asked when they were clear of the village.

'God only knows. We must simply play it by ear,' Basil replied. 'The main thing is to have as many options for entertaining her as possible.'

'Well anyway, the weather seems set fair for once. I'll take her round the grounds after tea and spin it out as long as possible. With Henrietta and Jeremy coming supper should be O.K.'

They arrived at Shirborough station in good time, and managed to park close to the main exit, sitting in the car until the approach of the London train was announced. It was drawing up as they went through the barrier and a large number of passengers began to disembark.

'You'd better stay here,' Basil told Amanda at the barrier. 'I'll go a bit further along. Look out for a shortish, middle-aged woman wearing something pretty ghastly.'

He vanished into the crowd. The cavernous roof of the station echoed the noise of shouted conversations, hurrying and shuffling footsteps and the hissing of the stationary diesel. Suddenly she caught sight of her father carrying a suitcase and a basket from which a thermos flask and a tin protruded. A middle-aged woman in a stridently blue suit walked beside him. She went forward to meet them.

'Here's my daughter Amanda, Laura,' Basil said.

'Hallo, Aunt Laura!' Acting on impulse Amanda stooped to drop a kiss on the expressionless face, aware as she did so of the surprise her action evoked. 'I'm Mandy to the family,' she went on. 'I'll take over the basket Daddy . . . The train must've been horribly hot and stuffy, I'm afraid.'

'Packed,' Laura Raymond replied tersely. 'People going off on holiday from the look of 'em.'

They went out into the station forecourt. Basil led the way to the car, remarking that it was luck to get a parking space so near. He unlocked the boot and deposited the suitcase inside.

'Let's have the basket too, Mandy,' he said. 'Now then, you sit beside me, Laura, and Mandy can go in the back.'

Doors slammed. A few moments later the Hyperion began to edge out of the parking slot.

'What's your car, Aunt Laura?' Amanda asked in an attempt to break the constrained silence.

'Second-hand Mini.'

'Mine's a Mini, too. But it's in a poorish way. To start with, I learnt to drive on it. Then I was in France for nearly a year, and standing in a garage doesn't do a car any good. My fiancé's got a pretty decrepit Mini, too, so we've decided to trade them both in and get something else to go off on our honeymoon in.'

As Laura showed no inclination to discuss Amanda's forthcoming marriage Basil reverted to the subject of cars.

'I can see you're interested in this box of tricks,' he said, and proceeded to point out the particular refinements of the Hyperion.

Laura relaxed and asked some questions.

'You could drive her at a moment's notice,' Basil told her. 'I can see you've got the hang of it. I won't suggest you take over now as I'm sure you're dying for a cup of tea, but you shall have a go tomorrow.'

'I'd like that,' she said, her tone gruff but indicating pleasure.

Once out of Shirborough the Hyperion gathered speed. They were well ahead of the rush hour and traffic had not yet begun to build up.

'Hardly worth taking the coast road short-cut, I should think,' Amanda remarked as they approached the turn-off.

'Not with traffic as light as this,' Basil agreed as they shot past.

The moment passed. In what seemed a short time they drew up in front of Loxford House. Basil got out and went round to open the door for Laura.

'I'll just take up your case,' he said, 'and put the car away.'

'Benny – Mrs Bennett, Daddy's housekeeper – will wash out your thermos,' Amanda told her, collecting the basket. 'Come along in and meet her, Laura.'

Mrs Bennett had been briefed by Basil and reacted suitably, running an eye over Laura's vivid blue suit, while expressing hopes that she would enjoy her visit.

'You'll be glad of a cup of tea, Miss,' she said, 'after being in a stuffy train. I'll bring it in in ten minutes, Miss Amanda.'

'Thanks, Benny. I'm dying for one myself. This way, Laura. I've put you next door to me, and we share the bathroom and loo along here . . .'

Laura Raymond glanced round her attractive bedroom but made no comment. Amanda told her not to hurry.

'Come downstairs as soon as you're ready, and we'll have tea. There's plenty of time to get into something cooler if you'd like to, after that hot train.'

She found her father in the drawing-room.

'Heavy going,' she remarked. 'She's a bit overpowered, I think, and reacting rather aggressively by saying nothing. You know. I'll take her round the garden after tea, and dinner will be much easier with Henrietta and Jeremy both here.'

Mrs Bennett entered with a tea-trolley, saying that she had got the kettle on the boil if more hot water was wanted.

'Good,' Amanda said. 'Leave the door half-open, Benny, so we can hear Miss Raymond coming down.'

Five minutes elapsed, punctuated by the steady ticks of a handsome grandfather clock. Suddenly there was a faint sound overhead. Basil jerked back his head and listened.

74

'My bedroom,' he said. 'She's having a bloody good snoop round. Go and get her, Mandy. The tea won't be fit to drink much longer.'

Reflecting that the week ahead was going to be far more demanding than she had expected, Amanda walked firmly across the hall. As she did so Laura appeared at the top of the staircase.

'I turned the wrong way when I came out of my room,' she said. 'I'm not used to mansions like this. Sorry if I've kept you waiting for your tea.'

'No problem,' Amanda assured her. 'Come along down.'

From quite an early age she had discerned, almost unconsciously at first, her father's capacity to present himself in whatever role he felt a situation demanded. Over tea he was the head of the family making an unexpected new member of it feel at home. He told Laura about various Railsdon cousins, and went to the length of fetching some snapshots from his study. Laura listened attentively, asking an occasional question and becoming slightly more expansive herself. When tea was over Basil suggested that Amanda should show her the garden if she were not feeling tired after her journey.

'Gracious no, I'm not tired,' she replied. 'Why, I've been sitting in the train for hours.'

As they strolled out of doors Amanda quickly realised that her aunt knew nothing about Georgian or any other type of domestic architecture, and could hardly distinguish one species of tree from another. Flowers proved a more successful topic. It appeared that the house at Medstone had a small garden. But surprisingly Laura showed considerable interest in Loxford village, and they stood looking down at it from the hillside behind the house. Amanda pointed out the church and the vicarage, explaining that it was the home of her fiancé's parents.

'I suppose your Dad owns most of the cottages down there?' Laura asked.

'Oh, no. He doesn't own any property locally except the farm over there and its land,' Amanda replied, pointing in a southerly direction where a cluster of buildings could be seen in the distance.

'Doesn't the lady he's going to marry live in the village?'

'Yes, she does. That's her cottage, over there, just beyond our meadow.'

'What's going to happen to it when she moves into your place, then?'

'She and Daddy are giving it to Jeremy and me as their wedding present.'

'Why, are you going to live here, too, when you're married? What's your boyfriend's job, unless he's got enough to keep you without working?'

Nettled by Laura's tone Amanda flushed slightly but managed to control herself. She replied that Jeremy taught at Mallingham College, and was moving to a new job at Oxford in January.

'The job is for the next three years. We shall have a small flat in Oxford for term-time, and come down to the cottage for the holidays.'

Laura began to speak but apparently thought better of it and broke off. Returning towards the house they passed the feedstore, a brick building with its wide door propped open with a stone and Basil's Hyperion visible inside. Amanda explained that at one time the family had had their own dairy cows, and food for them was kept in the store. Laura stood gazing at the Hyperion.

'A cut above my second-hand Mini,' she commented, 'and yours, too, from what you say.'

'Daddy has to have a car that gets over the ground. He often goes up to London on business, you see, and now he's been adopted as the next Conservative candidate for this area it means going to meetings and whatever . . . There isn't much room, but if you don't mind squeezing past the Hyperion you might like to see the weathercock that's going to be put up over the stable block.'

'Don't mind if I do,' Laura replied. As they managed to make their way to the back of the store she peered critically into the car, obviously more interested in its dashboard and gears than in the weathercock unwrapped for her inspection.

'Perhaps you'd like to unpack and have a rest now?' Amanda suggested as they emerged. 'Henrietta and Jeremy are coming in for a drink before supper somewhere between seven and half-past.'

Contrary to Amanda's expectations, the presence of two extra people appeared to make Laura more uncommunicative rather than less. Basil introduced an atmosphere of unreality by overplaying the role of the welcoming head of the family, and even Henrietta's charm and tact could only extract monosyllabic replies. It seemed that Laura was unable to make a contribution to a general conversation on the most commonplace of topics. While she admitted to having read about Jeremy Crabbe's recent achievements in the paper she showed no further interest, and looked appalled when he offered to take her to see Aretê Overton's official grave.

'Not to worry, step-aunt-in-law,' he told her in an attempt at jocularity. 'It's been closed up again, you know.'

There was no response. Henrietta hastily interposed by asking what plans there were for Laura on the next day.

Before anyone could answer the telephone rang.

'Probably for me,' Basil said, getting up and going out of the room with obvious relief.

'Let's hope it isn't Connie,' Amanda said. 'If it is, bang go twenty minutes at least . . . James Conibeer,' she explained to Laura, 'the present M.P. He's past it, and ought to have packed it in ages ago. He's always ringing up for advice, and now constituents have started buttonholing Daddy and writing to him.'

In the event Basil Railsdon reappeared in a couple of minutes.

'A nuisance,' he said. 'Tom Whitworth, my tenant farmer, wants to see me urgently about a contract he's been offered by a canning firm. He's got to ring them by midday tomorrow, so I had to tell him to come round at ten. I was just on the point of asking you if you'd like to come for a good run in the car tomorrow morning, Laura, and now we'll have to start a bit later.'

'In the Hyperion?' she asked.

'Sure.'

'Laura's fallen for her,' Amanda said. 'I could tell by the way she looked at her in the feedstore this evening.'

'I'd like a drive in her all right,' Laura replied, for the first time showing some enthusiasm.

'Nice job, isn't she?' Basil replied. 'Look here, Laura, going back to what we were saying on the way home, I'll take you along and show you the works presently, and you can bring her round at half-past ten tomorrow. And if you feel happy with her you could have a go on a fairly quiet road.'

'Oh, well, I don't know about that. Anyway, I'd like just to drive her round to the front door. Thanks a lot.'

Soon after this the supper party began to break up. Henrietta had come by car and offered Jeremy a lift to the vicarage.

'Thanks awfully,' he said, 'but I'll walk home, I

78

think. A spot of exercise and fresh air may clear my brain. I'm sweating over the ground plan of *The Overton Enigma* at the moment. Come as far as the gates, Mandy.'

After Henrietta had driven off Basil and Laura started for the feedstore, and Jeremy and Amanda strolled down the drive.

'Daddy's simply falling over himself to make poor old Laura feel she's one of us, isn't he?' she remarked.

Jeremy agreed.

'A note of reservation sticking out a mile. Why?'

'Oh, I don't know really. A bit overdone, perhaps?'

'You and Daddy are temperamentally poles apart. You're you. Always. He's any number of people, depending on who he's with. A useful knack in public life, I suppose. Jeremy, you don't think we'll have schizophrenic young, do you?'

'No, darling. Scrub the idea,' he replied, putting his arm round her and kissing the top of her head. 'I want them to be just like you. Immovably sound *au fond* with fascinating surface variations.'

'Lumme,' she murmured happily, resting her head on his shoulder.

They moved on slowly, discussing *The Overton Enigma.*

*   *   *

On the following morning, aware that Mrs Bennett was secretly averse to waiting on Laura Raymond, Amanda prepared a breakfast tray herself and took it upstairs just before nine o'clock. She found Laura awake and gruffly appreciative.

She then went to the dining-room and was consuming orange juice, toast and coffee when her father appeared, shortly followed by Mrs Bennett with bacon and eggs. They discussed plans for the afternoon and evening, and she then departed by car to keep an appointment with her hairdresser in Mallingham and do some shopping there. Basil finished his breakfast as the post van arrived at nine-thirty and went off to his study with his letters. Apart from domestic noises and intermittent hammering from the stable block the house was very quiet. Just before ten o'clock he heard Tom Whitworth's Land Rover coming up the drive and went to the front door to greet him and escort him to the study. They were soon deep in discussion of the pros and cons of the canning firm's offer.

Quite suddenly they both looked up abruptly at the sound of running footsteps crossing the hall. The door burst open and a white-faced Henrietta Legge came into the room.

'Come quickly, Basil,' she said urgently. 'It's Laura. She's had some sort of accident. In the feedstore.'

Both men leapt to their feet and ran out of the house.

'Good God, what *can* have happened?' Basil exclaimed as they sprinted down the path to the store. 'She started up the car several times last night to make sure she'd got the hang of it.'

They arrived at the store to find the big, heavy door wide open, the Hyperion as far forward as was possible without crossing the threshold, and Laura lying motionless beside it on the stone flags of the floor. Between them they lifted her up, carried her outside and laid her on a rug which Basil had snatched from the car.

'Christ!' Tom Whitworth exclaimed. 'Look at the colour of her face and her blue lips. Isn't that what carbon monoxide poisoning does? Shall I dash back to the house and put through a 999 call for an ambulance?'

80

'No,' Basil said, aware of Henrietta arriving at his side. 'Can you cope with that, darling? Good . . . Get your coat off, Whitworth, and we'll try artificial respiration.' As he spoke he pulled off his own and flung it down on the Hyperion's bonnet. 'She looks pretty far gone, but it's worth trying.'

They worked frantically, taking turns and assisted by Bill Cobbledick, hastily summoned from the roof of the stable block, but there was no response of any kind from Laura. Finally Basil stood up and wiped the sweat from his face.

'It's obviously no go,' he said. 'She's dead. What the bloody hell can possibly have happened?' He turned to Henrietta who had rejoined them, and was sitting on the grass looking badly shaken. 'How did you come to discover she was inside the store?'

'I came up over the meadow,' she told him. 'I wanted to try out some patterns of curtain material for my sitting-room now that the redecoration's finished. When I got near here I heard a car engine running, and then realised the sound was coming from inside the store and that the door was shut but not fastened. I never thought of the Hyperion being inside – I suppose I assumed you and Laura would be out in it by then. It must have been about twenty-five to eleven. I jumped to the conclusion that Bill had brought his van down for some more pantiles or the weathercock, and run back to the stables to fetch something, leaving the engine running, and that the door hadn't been propped open properly and swung shut. I thought I'd better open it because of the carbon monoxide building up, so I did. Then I saw Laura . . .' she shivered slightly. 'I fastened the door back and held the curtain patterns over my nose and mouth while I dashed in and switched off the Hyperion's engine, and ran to fetch you . . . I got through at once on 999,' she added, 'and the ambulance is coming as soon as they can make it.' She shivered again.

Basil looked at her and turned to Mrs Bennett who had by now joined the group.

'Benny, take Miss Legge back to the house and give her a stiff brandy. Look after her . . . Go along, darling. There's nothing any of us can do now but wait for the ambulance.'

When they had gone Basil stood gazing at the trees behind the feedstore.

'I suppose you can't see this place even from the top of the stable block roof?' he asked.

'No, that you can't,' Bill Cobbledick told him. 'And over to round an hour ago I was over on the north side, fixin' the last lot of pantiles. After that I was workin' on the old chimney down at the east end o' the roof ridge where we're puttin' the weathercock. I was down here with the van first thing to pick up the last lot o' pantiles and the weathercock, but everythin' was normal-like. Door shut and the Hyperion inside. Further back than she is now. I shut up again not knowin' if you'd be takin' the car out. I didn't know you 'ad a visitor.'

Basil went over to the Hyperion and picked up his coat. 'God, look at this!'

They all three stood staring at the radiator which showed signs of damage by impact.

'Looks as though the poor lady tried using it as a ram to force the door open,' Tom Whitworth suggested.

Examination of the inner side of the door showed marks at a height which seemed to bear out this idea. They were carrying out some rough measurements when Basil caught sight of an ambulance coming up the drive.

'I'd better go along and direct them straight here,' he

said. 'You two stay put. This place mustn't be left until the police have seen it. There'll have to be an inquest, of course.'

A few minutes later he reappeared, followed by the ambulance. The crew of two leapt out and knelt beside Laura Raymond's body. As another car could be heard Basil left the ambulance men with Tom Whitworth and Bill Cobbledick, and arrived at the front door as the police car drew up.

A youngish man got out and introduced himself as Sergeant Jones of the Crantshire Constabulary.

'Mr Railsdon, Sir?' he asked. 'Had an accident up here, haven't you?'

'Yes, we have. It's my half-sister who's staying with us, and how it happened God alone knows . . . It's just as quick to walk if you'd like to leave your car here.'

As they hurried in the direction of the feedstore with the constable driver bringing up the rear, Basil stated briefly that his sister had got trapped in a temporary garage in some inexplicable way, failed to turn off the engine of the car and appeared to have died from carbon monoxide poisoning.

'Three of us worked like hell till we nearly dropped at artificial respiration,' he said, 'but it was no use. She'd had too much of the bloody stuff.'

They arrived to find the ambulance crew lifting Laura on to a stretcher.

'We'll rush her back to Casualty at the Shirborough General, Sir,' the senior man told Basil, 'but frankly I don't think anything can be done. I understand she's a relative of yours? May we have her name? You'll get a ring from the hospital.'

A few moments later they drove off, and Sergeant Jones took over.

'I'm going to leave Constable Brown in charge here,

Sir,' he said, 'I suggest you gentlemen come with me to the house where I'd like to put through a call to my superiors, and then take a preliminary statement from you, if that's convenient.'

'Of course,' Basil replied. 'You can have my study which has a telephone. Mr Whitworth is a busy farmer, so perhaps you could take his statement first?'

As they all walked over to the house Sergeant Jones asked who had discovered Miss Raymond in the temporary garage.

'My fiancée, Miss Henrietta Legge. We're being married in September and I'm having some minor alterations and re-decoration done, and she came up to match some curtain material. She lives in the village, and there's a short-cut over the meadow from her cottage to this house. She came that way, and so passed the temporary garage: the feedstore, we call it. Hay and so on used to be kept there when we had our own cows.'

'Where's Miss Legge now, Sir? I'll need a statement from her.'

'Resting somewhere in here, I hope,' Basil replied, leading the way into Loxford House. 'She was naturally quite badly shocked, and I asked my housekeeper, Mrs Bennett, to take her back and give her some brandy.'

'Quite, Sir. I'll bother her as little as possible. Meanwhile I'll just ring H.Q. and then have a word with Mr Whitworth to start with, as you suggested.'

Tom Whitworth, Bill Cobbledick and Mrs Bennett were speedily disposed of, and Basil joined Sergeant Jones in the study.

'About the deceased lady's next-of-kin, Sir?' the latter asked. 'Would that be yourself?'

'As far as I can tell you, yes, although I don't honestly know if we're legally related. I'd better give you

84

some details, I think,' Basil went on, seeing a puzzled expression appear on the Sergeant's face. 'Miss Laura Raymond was my illegitimate half-sister and, surprising though it may seem, I didn't know that she existed until a few weeks ago when I suddenly had a letter from her. I've got it here if you'd like to see it, together with her birth certificate and another enclosure.' Getting up, Basil took a bunch of keys out of his pocket, selected one and unlocked a drawer. He extracted a folder marked '*L.R. Correspondence*', and handed it over. Sergeant Jones studied the contents with a slightly furrowed brow.

'I take it you answered the letter?' he asked.

'Yes. A more or less formal acknowledgement to begin with, not unfriendly I hope, but saying that I must, of course, submit the relationship claim she was making to my solicitor. I did this, and he established that the facts she had given me were perfectly genuine. Here's my correspondence with him, if you'd care to see it.'

Basil got up once more and extracted a second folder from the drawer. It was labelled '*Walker: Personal*'. After Sergeant Jones had read the letters it contained it was clear that he was feeling out of his depth.

'As our people will need to contact the police at Miss Raymond's normal place of residence,' he said, 'it will save time if I take over these documents now, Sir, and pass them on to whoever is put in charge of the enquiry into her death. I'll give you a receipt for them, of course.'

'Fair enough,' Basil replied. 'As I've explained, I've next to no knowledge of her home affairs. Who her solicitor is, for instance, if she had one.'

Sergeant Jones wrote out and signed a receipt for the two folders and their contents and put them into his brief-case.

'And now, Sir, if it's convenient, I'd like a word with Miss Legge – if she's up to it, that is.'

'Right. Just hold on a minute, will you, and I'll go and see how she is.'

A couple of minutes later he ushered Henrietta into the study, introduced Sergeant Jones and left them together. The latter drew up a comfortable chair for her.

'I'd like to say how sorry I am, Madam, that you've had such an unpleasant experience,' he told her, 'and sorry, too, to have to bother you with questions.'

Henrietta, pale but composed, smiled at him.

'Thank you, Sergeant. Just go ahead. I'm all right now.'

'I'd like you to tell me briefly how you came to find Miss Raymond in the – feedstore it's called, I think – and what immediate steps you took.'

His opinion of Henrietta rose steadily as she explained simply and clearly how she had become involved in the discovery.

'You showed great presence of mind, Miss Legge,' he assured her, 'and did absolutely the right things. Now just a couple of questions and I'll be through. Am I right in saying that the feedstore door isn't fitted with a lock, but that a staple and hasp are on the outside to keep it closed?'

'Yes, that's correct.'

'When you opened it this morning on hearing a car engine running inside the building was the staple hooked into the hasp?'

'No,' Henrietta replied without hesitation. 'I'm absolutely certain that it wasn't. You see, I grabbed hold of the staple which was hanging loose to pull the door open, and then pushed the door outward, if you follow me.'

86

'That's perfectly clear,' he told her, 'and leads to one more question, I'm afraid. Was it difficult to get the door wide open as you said you did?'

'It's a fairly heavy big door as you will have noticed. But if you mean did it jam or – well, resist being pushed open, no. Not in the least.'

'Thank you, Miss Legge. You've been most helpful,' he told her, making a few notes. 'I needn't keep you any longer.'

Crossing the room he held the door open for her to pass through and followed her into the hall. At the same moment Basil Railsdon emerged from the drawing-room.

'Come back in here and sit down, darling,' he said to Henrietta. 'Sergeant, your chap down at the feedstore – would it be in order to send along some sandwiches and a cup of tea?'

'I'm sure he'd appreciate it very much, Sir. I'm going back to H.Q. now, and you'll be getting a ring from us as soon as it's been decided which of the senior officers is to take over the enquiry into Miss Raymond's fatal accident. I . . .'

He broke off as a car drew up at the front door. Amanda got out, gathered up an armful of parcels and came quickly into the house, looking enchanting in green and white summer separates with her golden hair shining from her hairdresser's ministrations.

'Police car on the doorstep!' she exclaimed gaily. 'What have you lot been up to while I've been out?'

At the sight of her father's face her expression suddenly changed.

'Something's wrong. What is it?' she demanded.

'My daughter Amanda, Sergeant,' Basil said. 'I'm afraid there's been an accident, darling. Henrietta will tell you about it: she's in the drawing-room . . . I'm busy just for a few minutes . . .'

As she disappeared, followed by Sergeant Jones's eyes, the latter turned to Basil.

'Has Miss Railsdon been around here this morning?' he asked.

'She took up a breakfast tray to Miss Raymond about nine o'clock and was having her own meal in the dining-room when I came down at about a quarter past. She finished before me and went off in her car to Mallingham about nine-thirty to keep an appointment with her hairdresser, and seems to have been shopping afterwards.'

'Well, I'll be on my way, Sir.'

After the police car had driven off, Basil went to the drawing-room to find a tearful Amanda being comforted by Henrietta.

'Sorry,' Amanda said, drying her eyes. 'It's made me go all emotional. Such an awfully cruel thing to happen. All right, I know she'd have been a pain in the neck to tote around as one of the family but she'd had a rotten life up to now . . . I think I'll go and ring Jeremy.'

Chapter Five

The passage of an ambulance through Loxford shortly followed by a police car brought many people out of their homes. It was soon discovered that both vehicles were up at Loxford House and speculation was rife as the ambulance returned and made off towards Shirborough. When Bill Cobbledick came home for his dinner just after twelve-thirty, his van was besieged by enquirers. In the gruff and taciturn manner people had learnt to expect since his family tragedy he announced that a lady staying up at the House had somehow got herself shut into the feedstore with the engine of Mr Railsdon's car running and must have lost her head. Anyway she hadn't switched off the engine and was poisoned by the fumes. There'd have to be an inquest, so the police had turned up. Declining to give any further information about who the lady was and who had found her, he disappeared into his house.

The news of the disaster soon spread beyond the village. Basil Railsdon had to get up several times from the rather scratch lunch assembled by a shaken Mrs Bennett to answer telephone calls from friends living in the neighbourhood. He kept the conversations as brief as possible, explaining that he was expecting the police

89

to ring him. In the dining-room, Henrietta and Amanda pecked at their food during his absences, and repeatedly returned to the sheer incredibility of what had happened.

'That was Hugh and Jill Emsworthy,' Basil said on coming back for the third time. 'Well-meant, of course. Every time I pick up the bloody receiver I expect Jim Broadbent to be licking his lips at the other end.'

'What are you going to say to the press and the media about the relationship?' Henrietta asked.

'The only possible line's the truth, the whole truth, etc. Better to be perfectly frank about Father's goings-on than to have them ferretted out by newshounds. Times have changed, of course. I shall try a lightish man-to-man touch.'

'If only that bobby wasn't stuck down at the feed-store we could go and vet the door,' Amanda said after a pause. 'It simply must have jammed somehow. On quite a small stone that had somehow got wedged underneath, for instance, and jerked clear when she crashed the car against the inside of the door.'

'If you've both finished,' Basil said, 'I'll go and sit in the study near the phone. Fix Henrietta up comfortably in the garden, Mandy, and see if you can get Benny on to some coffee.'

'O.K.,' she said. 'I'll bring you in a cup. Jeremy's coming up when they've finished lunch.'

'You'd better stay around in case the police want a formal statement from you.'

*   *   *

The call from Shirborough police headquarters came through at half past three.

'Mr Basil Railsdon?' enquired a voice.

90

'Speaking.'

'Would you hold the line, sir?'

There was a brief pause followed by a click.

'Detective-Inspector Blair here, Sir. We've met before, if you remember, over the enquiry into Pippa Cobbledick's disappearance?'

'Oh, yes. You came along here in connection with my statement over the phone, didn't you?'

'That was it, Sir. Well, as things have turned out I've been put on to the enquiry into the unfortunate accident to Miss Laura Raymond on your property. To begin with, the Shirborough General Hospital has officially stated that she was dead on arrival, and a preliminary inquest into the cause of her death has been arranged with the Coroner for ten o'clock on Friday morning.'

'Thanks for letting me know, Inspector. It will be purely for purposes of identification, I take it?'

'For that, and for the issue of the burial certificate. You're prepared to identify her, I take it? Then we shall ask for an adjournment to allow the usual enquiries to go ahead.'

'Yes, of course I'll identify her. The burial question's a bit dicey . . . Can I take it that you've seen the various documents I handed over to Sergeant Jones this morning?'

'Yes, we've studied them here, and are contacting the police in the Medstone area for further information about her. It's a very unusual situation as I'm sure you agree.'

'I certainly do. When I met her in London she repeated the categorical statement that she had no other living relatives, but she may have had friends who would want to attend her funeral. If you get on to any through the Medstone police, I'd be grateful if you'd let me

91

know. Both my daughter and I want her to be buried here at Loxford as several generations of the family are.'

Inspector Blair undertook to pass on any relevant information.

'In the meantime, Mr Railsdon,' he went on, 'I'm afraid I must bring along a couple of technicians to have a look at the building and the car involved in Miss Raymond's death, and go through the statements you and others made to Sergeant Jones this morning. We can be with you by half past four if that's convenient?'

'Perfectly convenient. Everyone questioned by Sergeant Jones this morning is here at the moment except my farmer tenant, Tom Whitworth, and the farm's next door.'

'We'll start for Loxford right away, then, Sir.'

After ringing off Basil sat on at his desk for a couple of minutes, frowning heavily as he thought. Then he went out into the garden. Henrietta, Amanda and Jeremy were sitting in a group under a tree reading newspapers and magazines in a desultory fashion. As he approached they looked up at him enquiringly.

'A posse from the Shirborough C.I.D. are arriving at 16.30 hours to visit the scene of the crime and grill us all yet again,' he told them. 'The preliminary inquest's at ten o'clock on Friday morning. I suggest we have an early cup of tea now, before they arrive.'

'Shall we go and collect it on a tray?' Amanda asked, 'Or would you rather go indoors, Henrietta?'

'Let's stay out here, unless anybody feels strongly about it,' Henrietta said.

When Amanda and Jeremy had gone into the house she looked thoughtfully at Basil.

'Did Broadbent ring too?' she asked.

'Yes. I hope I handled him skilfully, but of course, as the blighter pointed out, I'm newsworthy these days.'

92

'What is particularly worrying you?' she stretched out a hand to him. He took it and held it in both his own.

'In the first place, Mandy's theory of the wedged stone seems to me to stretch probability a bit too far. In the second, the police will inevitably consider the possibility of somebody having come along, once she had started up the Hyperion's engine, slammed the door, and secured it by simply hooking the staple into the hasp affair.'

'But Basil,' Henrietta sat staring at him, 'how on earth could they assume she wouldn't have the wits to switch off the engine? And anyway, who on earth would have done such a thing? It isn't as if there are any children around who might have done it for a joke.'

'I don't know the answer to your first question. As to the second one, the police will be more interested in "could" than "would". I haven't a watertight alibi between roughly half past nine and ten, love. I was dealing with my letters in the study.'

'When did Laura go along to get the Hyperion?'

'I don't know. Mandy took her up a breakfast tray at nine, apparently. I never heard Laura come down, but Benny says she wasn't in her bedroom at ten to ten when she – Benny – went up to collect the tray.'

'You realise, I suppose, that I haven't an alibi at all? No one came to the cottage before I started off with the curtain patterns. I could have come unobtrusively up the meadow and watched from behind the feedstore till Laura arrived. And I knew she was coming alone to get the car out. We'd discussed it last night. Then I could have shut her in, and be lying about finding it unfastened.'

'Here's your own objection back again. How could you possibly have known that she'd go to pieces and leave the engine running? How could Benny have known, or Bill Cobbledick, or anyone in the world for that matter? Tea's coming. Change the subject, don't you think?'

The police car came up the drive with rather unnerving punctuality at four-thirty precisely. As Basil Railsdon got up from the group under the tree and went towards it, Detective-Inspector Blair extracted himself from the front seat. They greeted each other and shook hands, but it was perfectly apparent to Basil, although subtly conveyed, that this was a different type of encounter from their earlier one. Meanwhile two young men got out of the back of the car and began to collect various cases and types of camera from the boot. They were introduced as Detective-Constables Parker and Harris, a fingerprint expert and a photographer respectively. The driver, another constable, also got out, and joined them after locking the car. Inspector Blair turned to Basil.

'We're all complete now, Sir, if you'd kindly take us along to the building where the accident happened.'

Basil escorted the group along the grassy track leading to the feedstore. As they approached, Constable Brown rose from the chair provided for him and saluted Inspector Blair. The latter stood for several moments studying the exterior of the building. It was obviously old, built of mellowed brick in need of some repointing. The roof of slates was thickly encrusted with yellow lichen. Blair estimated the width as about twelve feet and the depth as approximately twenty feet. Much of the stone floor seemed to be occupied by the Hyperion, but there was uncluttered space behind the car. The stout wooden door, painted black, was wide open, propped by a large stone as Henrietta had left it that morning. There was no sign of the usual garage

94

clutter – tins, tools, rags and the miscellaneous junk invariably accumulated by car owners. There were no windows. In the past, ventilation had been provided by a couple of iron gratings in the side walls, now caked with rust and dirt.

Puzzled, Blair asked if this was where the Hyperion was always housed.

'Oh, no, we hardly ever use the place these days except to dump things like the pantiles I picked up last year,' Basil replied. 'She's only here to be under cover while the stable block which takes three cars is being re-roofed. Bill Cobbledick, our Loxford builder – you'll remember him, of course – is doing the job, and it's unfortunately behind schedule because of his family trouble. Otherwise, of course, this disaster wouldn't have happened.'

Blair made an assenting sound.

'Well, Sir, we needn't keep you waiting about here while we have a look round. I take it you and the other members of the household will be available shortly?'

'Yes, both of them, and Miss Legge is here. Bill Cobbledick is working late this evening to try to finish up. If you follow the track which goes round this place it'll bring you out at the stable block behind the house where he's working.'

With this, and with the sense of having received a very definite *congé*, Basil turned and went up the track towards the house. As soon as he was out of earshot Blair told his two technicians to start on the door.

'Don't move it,' he said, 'but I want it tested for prints inside and out. Deceased was a short woman – five foot two – so any dabs of hers trying to push it open from inside will be fairly low. But whoever slammed it on her from the outside was almost certainly taller. Do the jambs, and the staple and hasp, of course, but we can't hope for anything there as they're rusty and this Miss Legge who found her handled the staple, she says. You two others search round the outside for any signs of somebody having hung about watching for her to go in. I'm going along to have a word with the builder when I've had a look at those gratings from inside.'

Having satisfied himself that the gratings were inoperative, and had not been disturbed since they were put in, he started off. The track going round the back of the feedstore led on under trees to a cobbled space behind Loxford House. On the far side of this was a long, low building, originally stables and recently re-roofed with pantiles. A couple of ladders led up to a chimney at the eastern end, against which a small platform of planks had been constructed. A man was standing on this, occupied in securing a handsome weathercock to the chimneystack. Inspector Blair walked to the foot of the first ladder.

'Mr Cobbledick,' he called. 'I'd like a couple of minutes with you. May I come along up?'

Bill Cobbledick looked down in some surprise.

'Best I come down. We don't want no more accidents.'

Inspector Blair assured him that he spent his annual leave climbing in North Wales and the Lake District, and within a minute was at Bill Cobbledick's side. A quick glance confirmed that the feedstore could not be seen from the roof of the stable block when the intervening trees were in leaf.

'Obviously you couldn't have seen any comings and goings down there this morning,' he said, 'but I thought it was worth asking you if you remembered hearing the engine of the Hyperion starting up, or any unusual sounds.'

'Can't help you there either. Runs like silk, that engine does, and I was down the far side o' the roof, fixin' the last pantiles when Mr Railsdon came hollerin' for me.'

'Thanks, Mr Cobbledick. That's another point cleared up. We're asking everybody who was on the premises this morning to have their fingerprints taken, so will you contact my chaps down at the feedstore before you go home?'

'I'll do that.'

Inspector Blair glanced at the set unhappy face.

'Sorry to have had to turn up again, bringing back the past,' he said.

'You can't bring back what's still there . . . Reckon you people did what you could.'

Realising that his absence was preferable to his company, Inspector Blair descended the ladder, paused briefly to estimate the distance between the stable block and the back of the house, and saw a figure in a white overall move across what was obviously a kitchen window. He then returned to the feedstore.

A considerable number of fingerprints had been brought up on the inner surface of the door and were being photographed. Most of these were the result of vigorous pressure and made by a woman below average height. They were partly superimposed on less clear masculine prints, and near the outer edge of the door was a single set of prints made by a woman taller than the first one . . . Raymond, Railsdon, and probably Miss Legge, Blair thought as he contemplated them.

'When you're through with this lot get on to the inside of the car,' he told the two technicians, 'and don't muck it up more than you can help. It's a real top-notcher. You two others come up to the house and go through the stuff in the deceased's bedroom. Look

97

out for a diary or any letters. It's a hundred to one against you finding anything that ties up with this business, but it's got to be put on record that we searched. Then I'll tell Mr Railsdon that you'll take his dabs and the two ladies' and the housekeeper's. Nothing doing alongside this building anywhere, I take it?'

'Traces of a four-wheeled vehicle coming and going a fair number of times along the track you took, Sir, but nothing else,' Constable Brown reported. 'We've been over the ground in front here that the door passes over when it's opened and shut, and there's no sign of any bits of stone big enough to jam it.'

Basil Railsdon raised no objection to Laura's bedroom being searched. He took the constables up to it, and then escorted Inspector Blair to Mrs Bennett's little sitting-room.

'Please to take a seat,' she invited him as the door shut behind her employer. 'Not that I've anything more to tell you than I told the Sergeant this morning.'

Her eyes, bright behind old-fashioned gold-rimmed spectacles met his unwaveringly.

'What we are anxious to find out, Mrs Bennett, is when Miss Raymond left the house this morning.'

'That I can't tell you, as I said to the Sergeant this morning. She had her breakfast in bed. Miss Amanda took up the tray just before nine. I fetched it down again myself at ten minutes to ten. Wednesday's the day my morning help doesn't come, so I have to keep my eye on the clock. There was no answer when I knocked, so I went in. The bed was made and everything tidy, but nobody there.'

'Where did you suppose Miss Raymond had gone?'

'It passed through my mind that she'd gone out into the garden, seeing it was a nice morning, but I didn't give it much thought, to tell the truth.'

'You didn't think she was with Mr Railsdon?'

Over this enquiry Mrs Bennett was emphatic. She had seen Mr Railsdon take in the mail and go off to his study at half past nine, near enough. He'd shut the door and would be busy with his letters. He got a lot, and more than ever now he was going to stand for Parliament.

'I expect you were about just then clearing the breakfast things from the dining-room and taking them to the kitchen to wash up. You're quite certain you didn't hear anybody coming downstairs?'

'No, I didn't or I'd have said so. Mind you, I mightn't have heard if anybody had come down, with all the noise of hammering over to the stable block.'

Inspector Blair seized this opportunity to check on Bill Cobbledick's statement.

'Did the noise go on all the time?'

'Stop and go, every one or two minutes, from about half past eight. Enough to get on your nerves, but today'll see the end of it, thanks be.'

'Did you hear Mr Whitworth's car when he arrived to see Mr Railsdon?'

'Yes, I did, and Mr Railsdon came out of the study and over to the front door to bring him in. They went back there, and there they stayed till Miss Legge came dashing in to fetch Mr Railsdon. Just on twenty to eleven, that was.'

Feeling that nothing further was to be learnt from Mrs Bennett, Inspector Blair explained the necessity of taking specimen fingerprints from any member of the household who might have visited the feedstore during the past few months, and then left her. As he returned to the hall Basil Railsdon emerged from his study.

'Anyone else you want to see, Inspector?' he asked.

'There's just one matter arising out of your statement

to Sergeant Jones I'd like to take up, Sir, and one or two questions I'd like to ask each of the ladies.'

'Come along in here, then.'

The study was functional, with a huge kneehole desk, a cabinet file and a large bookcase, but it also offered two comfortable leather armchairs. Waved towards one of these, Inspector Blair sat down and took out a notebook.

'You'll understand, of course, Sir, that the Coroner will call for medical evidence at the resumed inquest on Miss Raymond. That's why we're anxious to establish the time at which she came downstairs this morning. It doesn't follow that she went straight to the feedstore, but it could relate to the time during which she was inhaling carbon monoxide, and this would affect the amount found in her bloodstream at the post-mortem. Did you by any chance hear her come downstairs to go out of the front door, either while you were finishing your breakfast, or after the mail van arrived and you brought your letters in here?'

'Not at either time,' Basil Railsdon replied without hesitation. 'Perhaps I'd better say that there was a certain amount of noise from the stables where Cobbledick is working, once I came in here, which might have prevented me from hearing her come down.'

Inspector Blair made another note and thanked him.

'Perhaps I could see the two ladies very briefly now?' he added.

'I think they're still in the garden. Would you rather see them in the house?'

'No need for that, Sir, if I can have a word with each of them separately.'

As they went out Amanda was coming towards the front door.

'Inspector Blair wants to speak to you,' her father

told her. 'I suggest you go and sit on that seat over there, and when he's through with you, take him along to Henrietta will you?'

Amanda was looking extremely attractive, still in her white and green outfit and with the evening sun glinting on her golden hair. Inspector Blair found himself obliged to make an effort to concentrate on his professional duty.

'Just one question, Miss Railsdon,' he said with formality. 'You remember taking up a breakfast tray to Miss Raymond this morning, of course?'

'Oh, yes. Perfectly well.'

'Was she up and dressed?'

'No. She was awake but still in bed.'

'This could be important. Are you quite sure that she had not got up and dressed and then gone back to bed?'

'Absolutely sure. You see, she sat up to take the tray and I registered a stout, sensible nightie.'

Inspector Blair was aware of amusement in her eyes and hastily dropped his own to his notebook.

'Thank you, Miss Railsdon . . . I see two of my colleagues coming downstairs, and they'll be asking if they can take your fingerprints when they've done your father's. You won't have any objection, I expect?'

'None whatever. It'll be a new experience. Shall we go along to Miss Legge now?'

He was introduced, and at Henrietta's invitation drew up a garden chair to sit facing her. His Super at Shirborough had briefed him sketchily on the people involved in the enquiry, and he had gathered that Henrietta was the last survivor of one of the real county families. They'd gradually lost their money and she now lived in a Loxford cottage. She had been engaged to a young officer in one of the crack regiments but he'd been killed in a car crash some years back. Doing a

101

good thing for herself in marrying Railsdon, the Super had added. Stinking rich he was, but a useful sort of bloke. He'd be the next M.P., no doubt about that . . .

'I'm very sorry to have to bother you, Miss Legge, after your upsetting experience,' Blair opened. 'I won't keep you long.'

She smiled at him, and he was aware of her charm and distinction.

'That's nice of you, Inspector, but go ahead. I know there must be an enquiry and you've got to have the facts.'

'Thank you, Miss Legge. As I've been saying all along the line, we are very anxious to find out the time when Miss Raymond left this house and went to the feedstore. You live quite near, don't you?'

'Yes. You can see a bit of my cottage if you stand up . . . It's that pink one, on the far side of the meadow.'

'Then you can see the feedstore from some of your windows?'

'Yes. The ones at the back.'

'Did you happen to look out that way before you came up here this morning?'

'Not consciously until a few minutes before I started, when I went to wash my hands in the bathroom. About twenty past ten.'

'And did anything strike you as at all unusual?'

'Only that the door of the feedstore was shut. You see, at supper last night it was arranged that Miss Raymond should bring the Hyperion round at half past ten, when Mr Railsdon thought he would have finished his business with Mr Whitworth and was going to take her for a drive. While he has been using the feedstore as a garage he hasn't bothered to shut the door after getting the car out until he puts it in at night.'

102

'What conclusion did you draw from the door being shut?'

'I don't think I really thought about it. It just passed through my mind that Miss Raymond must have already got the car out, and not knowing the drill, so to speak, just pushed the door to as one says, before driving off.'

'And there was no sign of anyone else about when you looked out?'

'I can say definitely that I didn't notice anyone.'

'Well, that's all very clear, Miss Legge, and thank you for your help. Was there anyone else in your cottage who might possibly have looked out of a back window earlier on this morning?'

'No, no one. I only have domestic help on Monday and Saturday mornings, and no guest staying with me at present.'

He thanked her again, asked for her cooperation in the matter of fingerprints, and went back to the two constables who were waiting in the drive outside the front door.

'When you've taken the lady's dabs come down to the feedstore,' he said, setting off towards it himself.

The technicians were waiting for him, lying on the grass. Blair stood for a few moments scrutinising the arc of ground over which the door passed in the process of being opened and closed. Coarse gravel had apparently been thrown down in front of the feedstore at some period and an attempt made to roll it in. Some pieces had worked loose in the course of time, and tufts of scrubby grass and weeds had established themselves.

'Right,' he said. 'We'll try opening and shutting the ruddy door, and see if it jams so that an average middle-aged female wouldn't have been able to force her way out.'

103

All three men experimented in turn, and agreed that, while moderately vigorous pushing was needed, there was no sort of jam that an ordinary woman in her forties could not have dislodged. At this point they were joined by the constables who had been taking Henrietta Legge's fingerprints.

'Get the door off its hinges now,' Blair told them, 'and we'll see if there are marks underneath of it being forced over something.'

The door was stoutly made of planks an inch thick, and heavy to manhandle. They managed to up-end and tilt it and inspect the bottom edge. This was dark with accumulated grime scored by about a dozen obviously recent scratches at different angles revealing relatively clean white wood. Blair gave a dissatisfied grunt.

'Railsdon said they were only using the place temporarily as a garage while the stables were being re-roofed. There no one scratch deeper than the others as though a lot of force had been used. Nothing conclusive here. We'd better have some close-ups all the same.'

While photography was in progress an exhaustive but unproductive search of the whole area near the door was made for any scored stone. As the technicians finally packed up Blair contemplated the pink cottage partly visible over the hedge at the far end of the meadow in front of the feedstore.

'O.K.?' he enquired, turning to his support. 'I must put in five minutes with this chap Whitworth on the farm next door, and then we'll be through.'

The visit to Loxford Farm confirmed that Basil Railsdon had come to the front door to meet Tom Whitworth at ten o'clock sharp that morning, and that they had gone to the study and discussed the canning factory's proposal and various other business matters until Miss Legge came running in at about twenty to eleven.

'I was just getting up to go,' the farmer said. 'Mr Rails-don was expecting a relative who was staying with them to bring his car round at half past ten so he could take her for a drive, and he thought he'd better go and find out what she was up to. We both dashed over to the feed-store, and I can only tell you that we went all out to get the lady round, with Bill Cobbledick taking his turn with the two of us. We couldn't have done no more.'

Inspector Blair assured him that it was daylight clear that they'd done everything possible, and managed to disengage himself.

*   *   *

At Loxford House Basil Railsdon's main preoccupation was the outcome of the police search of Laura's bed-room. Had, for instance, a diary been found in which the events on the coast road earlier that year were recorded? There was no means of knowing. One could only wait and hope for the best. If the worst happened the line to take would be that it was pure fantasy – wish-fulfilment arising from her deep-seated anger and resentment towards her father's family. In the meantime the obvious course was to act in a normal way for a half-brother who believed himself to be her only known relative.

He rang Miles Walker, broke the news of Laura's death, and asked if steps should be taken to find out if she had had a solicitor. She might have left instructions about her funeral, for one thing.

To his relief, Miles Walker replied that Laura had given him as a reference the name of a chap who had acted for her at the time of her mother's death and sub-sequently drawn up her own Will. There would be a record at the office.

'I'll ring the bloke as soon as I get to the office tomorrow,' he said, 'and tell him to contact you. Somebody should most certainly keep an eye on her house and other assets during the enquiry and until probate is granted . . . I'm damn sorry you've been landed with a situation like this, old man. If you hadn't been decent enough to ask her down it wouldn't have happened. It really is the most extraordinary situation. If the slightest suggestion of negligence or liability on your part arises, get in touch at once, of course, and we'll watch out for any potentially libellous publicity in the press or on the media. That sort of thing can be very profitable.'

Basil replaced the receiver with a wry smile, and picked up the copy of the *North Crantshire Evening News* that was lying on his desk. He read once again the reference to the disaster in the Stop Press column.

MYSTERY DEATH AT LOXFORD HOUSE
Miss Laura Raymond (46), relative of Mr Basil Railsdon, was found dead from carbon monoxide poisoning in a temporary garage this morning.

As a prelude to the inevitable publicity ahead it could have been a lot worse, he thought.

Miles Walker was as good as his word. Soon after ten the next morning a call came through from a Medstone solicitor who gave his name as John Webster, of Webster and Treat. He confirmed that he had acted for the late Mrs Elsie Raymond and after her death for Miss Laura Raymond. He had recently drawn up a Will for the latter. He expressed dismay at hearing of her death under such distressing circumstances, and while not in the same category as Miles Walker and his partners, he struck Basil Railsdon as reasonably competent and experienced. He undertook to contact the Medstone

106

police and go with them to the house if they wanted to inspect it. She had appointed himself as her sole executor, and he had just had a quick look at her Will. She had expressed a wish to be cremated, but none as to the disposal of her ashes. Mr Railsdon's suggestion that her ashes should be interrred in Loxford churchyard near those of other members of the family seemed to him, as executor, a very suitable one . . . Yes, Mr Walker had put him in the picture about Miss Raymond's parentage, although neither she nor her mother had ever mentioned it to him.

'The preliminary inquest is in Shirborough at ten o'clock tomorrow,' Basil informed him. 'Thank you for letting me know that she wished to be cremated. I'll pass that on. But I can't imagine any difficulty arising over the burial certificate. I suggest that I go ahead with the arrangements at this end and keep in touch with you. May I have your telephone number? Thanks,' he went on, after taking it down. 'If by any chance you would like to come down for the cremation, I'll meet your train and we could lunch at a Shirborough hotel.'

Not altogether to his surprise Mr Webster appeared to welcome this idea. He was clearly intrigued by the whole situation.

After thinking for a couple of minutes Basil decided to take the initiative of ringing Inspector Blair, his ears attuned to any nuance, however slight, in the latter's utterances. He was asked to hold the line by the switchboard operator at Shirborough police headquarters. After a short pause there was a click.

'Mr Railsdon? Inspector Blair speaking.'

'Good morning, Inspector. I hope I'm not being officious but I thought I'd let you know that I have managed to contact Miss Raymond's solicitor – a Mr John Webster of Medstone. I got on to him through my own.

107

It appears that Miss Raymond gave Mr Webster's name as a reference when she was being asked by my chap for proof of identity.'

'That's useful, Mr Railsdon. Thank you for letting me know. I'll pass the information to Medstone who may not have managed to get that far.'

'Mr Webster is the sole executor of Miss Raymond's Will. He told me that he had just looked it up, and found that she had expressed a wish to be cremated. Is it enough to let you know this, or ought I to contact anyone else? The signatures of two doctors are required on the death certificate in the case of a cremation, aren't they?'

'Yes, they are, but this won't cause any difficulty. One of our police surgeons did the post-mortem last night, and was assisted by another. They found that carbon monoxide poisoning was the sole cause of death. And by the way, as you probably know, there's quite a queue for the Crematorium these days. I think you would be well advised to get in touch with the funeral directors you will be employing. Quite in order to alert them today. I'll see you have the burial certificate after the inquest tomorrow morning.'

Basil Railsdon thanked him and they rang off . . . Satisfactory, he thought, reviewing the conversation. Matter-of-fact but easy, and even a touch of humour. It had been a good move to make the call. He roused himself to telephone the firm of funeral directors in Shirborough who had coped with his father's burial, and was at once put through to its senior partner.

The day continued busy but uneventful. The Regional T.V. company and a press agency rang to ask for interviews, and he complied with both requests, allowing the exterior of the feedstore to be photographed and posing himself in front of Loxford House.

Numerous calls came through from friends and acquaintances, and in the afternoon there was one from Ling and Grant, the leading firm of estate agents in Mallingham. A senior member of their staff had visited Abbey Cottage during the morning, and estimated its value at current prices for house property in the district as £30,000. Basil Railsdon proceeded to contact his stockbroker in London, and after discussion of market values and trends arranged for shares to the value of £25,000 to be transferred to Henrietta Legge. This done, he got out the Hyperion and drove over to see her. Over tea he described the steps he had taken towards transferring the ownership of the cottage to Amanda.

'You see, you're contributing £5,000,' he told her, 'making it a present from us both in terms of hard cash. The next step is to get the deeds put in Amanda's name. Are they with your solicitors or at the bank?'

Henrietta replied that they were with her other securities at her bank in Mallingham, and it was decided to have them sent to her solicitors there who were conveniently the same firm as that employed by Basil himself in matters of a purely local nature.

'I'll go over and see about it tomorrow morning,' she said, 'while you're at that wretched inquest. You're absolutely sure you don't want me to come with you?'

'Absolutely, darling. It's a pure formality, and Mandy insists on coming. The resumed inquest will be a different affair altogether, with all of us taking the witness stand in turn, I'm afraid.'

'When do you think it will come off?' she asked as she refilled his cup.

'I should think the police will ask for a week's adjournment, to give time for the Medstone police to collect up some gen about Laura. Not longer, I imagine.'

'Where is Mandy, by the way?'

'Acting as Jeremy's amanuensis at the County Records Office. He's collecting background information for this book of his.'

In actual fact the pair had knocked off in the early afternoon and gone for a bathe in a small bay a few miles on the far side of Shirborough. They were now sunbathing on the beach.

'Heaven, isn't it?' Amanda said. 'Another world from all the beastly business over poor Laura. I felt I simply must go and give Daddy moral support tomorrow.'

'Tomorrow won't be anything beyond running the gauntlet of newsmen's cameras when you're going in and coming out. The adjourned inquest's another matter. The police will have raked together every conceivable relevant fact as fodder for the Coroner's questions, and the local press at any rate will go to town on it all.'

'Shall I have to give evidence?'

'I shouldn't think it's very likely. They'll have checked with your hairdresser, for one thing.'

They basked in silence for a spell.

'Jeremy,' Amanda said suddenly, 'I've simply got to put it into words. It's what we're all thinking. I mean, it's easy to imagine Laura not fastening the door back properly with the stone, and that it swung shut again after she'd got into the car, and she found it had stuck on something when she got out and went to open it again. But suppose the sticking can't actually be proved? I opened up for Daddy the other day and didn't need to push much.'

'It's certainly odd enough to make the police go into it all pretty exhaustively,' he admitted. 'That's what I was thinking just now, actually. About Coroner's questions, I mean. She might have been acutely claustropho-bic, of course, and just gone to pieces when the door seemed to shut itself on her. If she was, the Medstone police will get on to it.'

'Let's say what else we're thinking. That somebody had it in for her, hid behind the door, gave it a push and hooked it shut.'

'Of course we've all been thinking that. But who could possibly have known that she wouldn't have the gump-tion to switch off the engine? That's what suggested to me that she might have been abnormal in some way – claustrophobically or otherwise. Because basically the whole business looks rather like a silly rag. If somebody did shut her in, they soon unhooked the door again. It was unhooked when Henrietta came along, wasn't it?'

'I feel a lot better now I've unbosomed myself to you,' Amanda said, slipping her hand into his.

'Time I married you, and stood between you and the harsh realities of life. Let's go in again, shall we?'

As they raced each other across the sand to the water's edge he wondered how she would react to the mention of two matters concerning her father which were still puzzling him. One was the speed with which Basil's atti-tude to their marriage had changed. The other was his obvious and surely excessive anxiety that Laura Ray-mond should enjoy her visit to Loxford House. Not in character, Jeremy thought, and wondered if it was remotely possible that she was trying to blackmail him. About something pretty unspeakable connected with his father, for instance . . .

*   *   *

The inquest on the following morning was as brief and straightforward as Inspector Blair had forecast. A week's adjournment for further enquiries into the cause of death was asked for by the police and granted by the Coroner. After exchanging a few words with the Inspector, Basil Railsdon emerged from the building with a hand under Amanda's elbow. He paused almost imperceptibly to face a battery of cameras, and parried a series of questions with practised skill. One or two were directed at Amanda, and he was gratified by her composure and adroitness in answering them.

The weekend brought a relaxation of tension and a reduction in the news coverage of what the local press and regional news were referring to as the 'Loxford House Garage Mystery Death'. By Sunday evening Basil Railsdon found himself able to give his undivided attention to urgent business matters. On Monday morning he drove the Hyperion to the garage in Mallingham with which he dealt to discuss the damage to the radiator. Henrietta accompanied him, and they went on to the solicitors who were to deal with the transfer of the deeds of Abbey Cottage to Amanda. Lunching at the hotel patronised by their social group they were greeted by numerous friends who expressed sympathy and support. Finally they drove back to Loxford in a car hired for the period of the Hyperion's repairs. There had been no telephone calls or visits from the police during their absence, and they relaxed over tea in the drawing-room with its french windows wide open to the garden. Pressed to stay on to supper, Henrietta replied that she really must go home.

'Still a few unanswered letters of congratulation,' she said. 'And now the deeds are being dealt with I ought to push on with sorting out my possessions.'

'I'll drive you round, of course.'

'Lovely. I'm ashamed to admit it, but I'm still a bit allergic to the short-cut over the meadow.'

'I'll have the bloody feedstore pulled down if you like. It's hardly ever used for anything these days. Come to think of it I'd be glad to get rid of it myself. The sight of it's bound to bring this wretched business back.' As she spoke he could hear approving comments . . . 'Railsdon had the shed place where it happened pulled down. I don't wonder, do you? The sight of it would always have given me the creeps . . .'

'Well, if you really feel that way,' Henrietta said. 'But I'm sure I'd get over my reactions in time.'

Basil drove her to Abbey Cottage, unlocked her front door for her and saw her inside with an affectionate kiss. He returned to Loxford House with a sense of well-being, driving round to the stable block where Bill Cobbledick had finished the re-roofing, and putting the car away in his usual garage. This done he stood for a moment contemplating the pleasing effect of the pantiles and the elegant weathercock. Appropriately the wind direction was indicated by a gilded galloping horse instead of the more usual cock. Caught in the rays of the late afternoon sun it appeared almost luminous. Apparently Amanda, who had been spending the day with friends on the far side of the county, had not yet returned, as the garage she was using was open and empty. His thoughts turned to having a drink. He went into the house by way of the back door, pausing for a word with Mrs Bennett. When the telephone rang he lifted the receiver without a tremor of anticipation, wholly unprepared for the blow that was to fall.

Chapter Six

Monday had also seen Detective-Chief Superintendent Pollard's return to New Scotland Yard after a fortnight's holiday spent with his family at the seaside. He found that an appointment had been made for him to report to his Assistant Commissioner at two o'clock.

When he presented himself he got an appraising glance.

'Afternoon, Pollard. No need to ask if you've had a decent break.'

'No, Sir. Really superb weather all through, and no hang-ups, major or minor.'

'Fine. Now then – ' The A.C. reached for a folder, opened it and ruffled through its assorted contents. 'Does Loxford, Crantshire suggest anything to you?'

'I'll say it does, Sir. That remarkable research by the vicar's son down there. They managed to get a Home Office permit to open a grave purporting to be that of the last Abbess of Loxford Abbey but one. No skeleton found, but a superb golden casket containing a reliquary. The V. and A. are restoring them.'

The A.C. looked at him with sardonic amusement.

'Right up your street, that sort of thing, of course. Well, Loxford has got itself on to the front pages again,

with what the Crantshire chaps are convinced i
der. The sort that looks like being impossible
and bring home to anybody. The victim was a
the illegitimate half-sister of a leading light in the
life of the county. He's called Basil Railsdon,
Loxford House, is rolling in money, and has ju
selected as prospective Tory candidate for
Crantshire at the next General Election. He cla
and there's some supporting evidence ¬ that he
know of her existence until about six weeks ago
she contacted him by letter. He invited her dow
stay and she arrived last Tuesday. The next mor
she was found dead from carbon monoxide poisoni
the sole cause of her death, the post-mortem found ¬
a building being used by Railsdon as a temporary ga
age. As far as the Crantshire C.I.D. have been able
discover, he was the only person in Loxford or an
where near who had ever met her before she can
down, apart from the woman who runs the village sho
who had sold her some postcards last May. Not unnat
urally they've got their sights on Railsdon and wonde
if she was trying to blackmail him. However, he's go
an alibi of a sort. Not the cast-iron type that arouse
instant suspicion, but the type that experienced Coun
sels can present as absolutely convincing or completely
valueless with equal facility. The reason why the buck
has been passed to us is that the Crantshire chaps know
that they're going to raise the hell of a stink whatever
they do. If they make out a case against Railsdon the
overwhelmingly Tory North Crantshire will go over the
top, especially as there seems to be a possibility of the
local woman he's about to marry being involved too.
There's also the possibility that the door was difficult to
push open from the inside and the woman just
panicked, and it's a non-case. And if they go for a ver-

ccidental Death the smaller, but vocal Left will
ing 'one law for the rich', etc.'
. stage are the legal proceedings at?' Pollard

adjourned inquest was due to be held next Fri-
hen we let them know a couple of hours ago that
ake on the case they put in an application for a
r week's adjournment . . . It's an interesting case
the look of it, even if the answer turns out to be a
n. You get far too many interesting cases, Pollard,
ve said before, but as you've nothing else of major
rtance on hand at the moment, you'd better go
n right away. Plus Toye, I suppose. We'll let police
). at Shirborough know that you're taking over, so
g them to say roughly when you'll arrive. Better take
se notes,' the A.C. concluded. 'You can read 'em on
e way down, and get some idea of the lie of the land.
d step on it. The sooner you and Toye get back the
tter.'
Dismissed with a brusqueness that did nothing to
ide the A.C.'s interest in the case, Pollard returned to
is own office. Here the routine had become familiar to
ne point of being automatic. Inspector Gregory Toye
ho had worked with him for not far short of twenty
ears was summoned, cursorily briefed, and departed
o organise transport and ring Shirborough. Urgent
left-overs in the in-tray were farmed out to subordi-
nates. A call was put through to Pollard's home in
Wimbledon. Everyone appeared to be out, and his personal secretary undertook to call the number at hourly
intervals, and assure Mrs Pollard that she would get a
ring from her husband at some time during the evening.
With a final glance round, Pollard picked up the folder,
his overnight case and murder bag, and went down in
the lift to the car park. As he expected, Toye was

116

already sitting at the wheel of the black Rover studying a route map.

'I'll start in the back,' Pollard told him. 'There's some quite useful gen in this folder to mop up. Then I'll come in front and pass it on.'

He settled himself into the nearside corner of the rear seat, stretching out his long legs diagonally. The contents of the folder were a simplified plan of Loxford as a whole, a list of the people who, on paper, could have been involved in Laura Raymond's death with a brief note on each one, and the timetable of events known to have taken place in and around Loxford House roughly between nine o'clock and noon on the previous Wednesday, August the third.

Pollard contemplated the map with interest. Although close to the village and probably visible from the main Mallingham-Shirborough road, Loxford House at the end of its drive was in one sense rather remote from it. The approach across the meadow from Abbey Cottage was not, apparently, a right of way as no footpath was marked from the end of the cul-de-sac where it was situated. Access to Loxford House was obviously possible from the north through the woods, and also from the Abbey Farm land on the east side of the drive. All these facts needed bearing in mind, Pollard decided.

He next studied the list of people compiled by the Shirborough C.I.D. All these would have to be re-interviewed at some length. And even if it could be established beyond any reasonable doubt that Basil Railsdon's first contact with his half-sister had been roughly two months ago, it would still be necessary to investigate her life in Medstone from childhood onwards. They would have to spend time there interviewing neighbours, friends, fellow employees and her employer.

The timetable for the period covering her death was

117

thought-provoking, he decided. It struck him forcibly that if Basil Railsdon's alibi had holes in it, his fiancée's was non-existent. At least Shirborough had made no mention of her presence at Abbey Cottage being confirmed by anyone. He turned back to the brief note on Henrietta Legge. '*Age 30. Unmarried but engaged to marry Basil Railsdon as his second wife in early September. Last surviving member of well-known county family. Highly thought of locally, but known to be hard up.*' Pollard allowed himself to speculate briefly that Laura Raymond had discovered that her half-brother had already made a second marriage, and was proposing to blow the gaff. This would lend support to Shirborough's suggestion of blackmail . . .

Pulling himself together he began to think about Mrs Bennett and her evidence. '*Age 61. Widow,*' her biographical note stated. '*Housekeeper at Loxford House since 1964. Previously on domestic staff of Ollsford Castle where her late husband had been one of the gardeners.*' Clearly, Pollard thought, it was Mrs Bennett's evidence – or non-evidence, if you like – that would make a case against Railsdon so dicey . . . Yes, she had seen Mr Railsdon go into his study just after the mail van had come up, and heard him shut the door . . . No, she had not heard him come out again before Tom Whitworth had arrived at ten o'clock . . . No, she had not heard Miss Raymond come down the stairs . . . But they might have been about, both of them. She'd been busy clearing away breakfast, and in the kitchen, and going upstairs to fetch down the visitor's tray . . . And then all the hammering on the roof of the stable block could have explained why she hadn't heard anybody . . .

Pollard wondered what type of employee she was. Faithful retainer, devoted to Basil Railsdon and his daughter? Tenacious of her position after long service and resentful of his impending remarriage to Henrietta Legge? Secretly 'left' and resentful of the family's wealth and social status? Anyway, he decided, she was down for some pretty intensive questioning.

They had got clear of London before the rush hour traffic began to build up and were making good headway. When Toye branched off the M3 Pollard told him to pull in to the next lay-by.

'We can spare a quarter of an hour,' he said. 'Briefing you will help me clear my head, and you might even come up with something. Who knows?'

A grin developed on Toye's pale and usually impassive face. Within five minutes they had pulled up. Pollard handed him the plan of Loxford.

'Get this stamped on your mind,' he told him, 'and I'll begin.'

Toye, whose passion in life was cars, had a strong subsidiary interest in maps and plans. After a couple of minutes he announced that he'd got the place taped.

'Right,' Pollard replied. 'Here goes. The top brass of Loxford is the owner of Loxford House, Basil Railsdon, a widower of forty-two, extremely well-heeled and about to make Miss Henrietta Legge of Abbey Cottage his second wife . . .'

Toye listened to the resumé without interruption. When it came to an end he sat for a full minute staring unseeingly at a vista of fields and woods through a gap in the hedge.

'I'm with you,' he announced finally. 'Bit out of the ordinary, isn't it, for a half-sister of forty-six to turn up like that out of the blue? In that walk of life, I mean?'

'Decidedly. However, Railsdon's London solicitor is a partner in a well-known top firm, and if he accepted the relationship as authentic after carrying out

119

enquiries I reckon we can take it as read. Has anything about the case struck you that I haven't mentioned?'

'Deceased must have had a car of her own, or anyway been a good driver. Railsdon would never have let her touch the Hyperion otherwise. Not a car in that class,' Toye affirmed, a gloating note in his voice. 'So what seems downright fantastic to me is that when the door shut on her she didn't automatically switch off the engine, seeing the place hadn't any windows. It's the reaction you'd expect from anybody who'd ever had anything to do with a car.'

'She could have been an hysterical type, I suppose, and simply lost her head and gone berserk. We'll see her doctor when we go to Medstone as well as her neighbours and the people she worked with. I wonder if some people are more susceptible to carbon monoxide poisoning than others, and she got dopey quickly? We'll talk to the medico who did the P.M. at Shirborough about that.'

'Say she was the hysterical sort who'd go to pieces, could some kid have shut her in for a lark and come back and unhitched the door fastening after a bit, not realising what had happened? Taking the noise of the engine as showing somebody was inside?'

'You might be on to something there,' Pollard said a little dubiously. 'We'll find out if Loxford has any juvenile delinquents. Also find out if there's anything in the way of a village idiot . . . Perhaps it's time we pushed on.'

Toye took the direct route to Shirborough, passing north of Mallingham and Loxford, and they arrived at police headquarters just before seven. The initial contact with a Chief Constable and his senior C.I.D. could be stiff, but on this occasion Pollard and Detective-Chief Superintendent Gregg immediately recognised each other, having been on a course together in their earlier days. This at once eased the atmosphere and encouraged uninhibited discussion over drinks produced from a cupboard in the Super's office. Gregg had changed very little in appearance, Pollard thought. Tall, dark and lantern-jawed with an habitually wary expression. Major Freeman, the C.C., was heavily-built and greying at the temples, with the impassive cast of face that gives nothing away. It was these two, Pollard felt sure, who had decided on calling in the Yard, while Inspector Blair was aggrieved at being deprived of the chance of carrying on. He sat a little apart, younger than the others, fair-haired and with an immediately unremarkable but intelligent face.

'Cheers,' Major Freeman raised his glass. 'Well, the balloon's gone up already. I've had that old windbag Conibeer on the line blowing his top. He's our sitting M.P. Somehow the local rag, the *Shirborough Evening News*, has got on to the Yard takeover. There wasn't time to reset the entire front page but they've managed to get in a para expressing amazement, and that's how Conibeer knew about it. I've told the switchboard to tell callers that neither senior C.I.D. officers nor myself are available at present.'

'Who told Mr Railsdon that we were coming in on the case?' Pollard asked.

'I did, sir,' Inspector Blair replied briefly and woodenly.

'What did you make of his reaction? Your opinion's valuable since I gather you've been on the case from the start.'

Thawing slightly, Blair said that Mr Railsdon had seemed stunned for a moment, and had then protested angrily about the additional objectionable publicity that he and his family and future wife would now have

121

to put up with. 'For what it's worth,' he went on, 'I got the feeling that he was properly scared.'

'From the look of things so far,' the C.C. said, 'he might well be. I take it you've seen the précis of the situation we sent up to the Yard with our application for a takeover, Mr Pollard?'

'Yes, I have, and it's been a great help. We're unusually well-placed for absorbing the complete case file. This had better be our first job, and then we'll decide on a plan of action.'

Superintendent Gregg came in with the information that a temporary office with a telephone had been organised, and accommodation fixed up at a nearby hotel. If wanted, a second car would be made available.

'That's fine,' Pollard said. 'We'll go along to our pub and have something to eat, and then come back and get down to the file. Just one more thing. May we take it that we can contact Inspector Blair when we feel it would help?'

'Of course you can,' the C.C. replied. 'I'm sure he'll be glad to cooperate, won't you, Blair? And he's done a damn good job on the case up to date. But of course we haven't the Yard's facilities down here. Then there's the Medstone end to cope with, too.'

Amende honorable, Pollard thought, as the conference came to an end.

It was nearly midnight before he and Toye agreed that they had absorbed the contents of the case file and were in a position to draw up a programme for the following day.

'As I see it,' Pollard said, scowling and ruffling up his hair, 'the first thing is to decide whether or not Raymond hadn't propped the feedstore door open properly and got apparently shut in by accident, panicked and forgot to switch off the car engine, and finally succumbed to carbon monoxide poisoning. Alternatively, did the door jam on something so that she actually couldn't get out – once again a case of accidental death. Let's have another look at the blown-up photographs of the underneath of the door.'

Sitting side-by-side they examined the photographs once again.

'Not a sign of the sort of real scrape a biggish bit of stone would have made,' Toye said. 'And Blair says, doesn't he, that they combed the place all around to find a stone with scrape marks on it? As to Raymond going berserk, we'll have to see her doctor in Medstone.'

'Write off the jam theory for the moment, then. What next? Your lark theory. Can we eliminate kids and village idiots? The best way to do this will be to call on the Loxford vicar. He's the father of Jeremy Crabbe who's engaged to Railsdon's daughter, isn't he? You never know what unexpected bit of info may come out in general chat. And if young Crabbe is available I'll tell him I'd like to run through the statement he made to Blair. He's an exceedingly bright lad and might come up with something. One can't tell how long all this will take. There might be time to pay a courtesy call on Railsdon and inspect the scene of the alleged crime. Anyway, we'll eventually fetch up in Mallingham, pool our findings and plan the afternoon programme.'

Toye, who had been listening attentively while re-assembling the contents of the file, agreed that it sounded the best way of getting started on the job.

'Right then,' Pollard said. 'Now we'll concentrate our thoughts on Basil Railsdon who seems to have been cast for the leading role by the Shirborough C.I.D., and who is in a good old tiz over our being brought in. Blair has been very thorough, and as things stand I can't see how Railsdon could have done the job on his own, especially in the light of the medical evidence. The doctors who did the P.M. say that from the amount of carbon monoxide in Laura Raymond's blood she must have inhaled the stuff over a period of about an hour or more, the time depending on the ventilation of the feedstore. If she was in bed in her nightie just before nine o'clock when Amanda Railsdon took up her breakfast tray, she could hardly have eaten or disposed of the food and coffee or whatever, dressed, and got round to the feedstore before nine-fifteen. This is the time when Mrs Bennet says she took in Railsdon's breakfast, presumably a cooked one which she had been keeping hot. The driver of the mail van told Blair that he was on time that morning, and handed over the Loxford House letters to Railsdon in person just after half past nine, and that Miss Railsdon passed him in her car going down the drive as he came up it. Mrs Bennett is very reluctant to commit herself, but she is quite definite that Railsdon went off to his study with his mail, shutting the door behind him. She says she didn't hear him come out again until Tom Whitworth's Land Rover arrived at ten o'clock, but adds that she was busy and the builder Cobbledick was making a row, and so she mightn't have. We must remember that the study is on the ground floor. Railsdon could perfectly well have got out of the window, gone round to the feedstore, lurked behind it until Laura Raymond appeared and went inside, slammed the door on her and fastened it as soon as he heard her start up the Hyperion's engine. Plenty of time for him to return via the study and wait for Whitworth's arrival. We know she had cleared off from her bedroom by ten minutes to ten. But he couldn't have gone back again to unhook the staple before Henrietta Legge arrived at the feedstore at approximately half past ten and found the door unfastened, could he?

'Looks as though the two of them could have been in it together,' Toye agreed. 'We've only her word for it that she found the staple hanging loose. And it allows about three-quarters of an hour for Raymond to be inhaling the fumes.'

'But how did either Railsdon or Legge know she wouldn't switch off the engine? That's the brick wall we're up against. Unless, of course, one or more of the supporting cast are lying about times. There's the hell of a lot of checking and counter-checking of statements ahead, old son. Let's pack it in now, though. Good Lord! To think that only last Saturday afternoon I was surfing with Jane and the twins.'

*   *   *

On the following morning they started early for Loxford. As they drove slowly through the village Pollard spotted a lane running off the main street on the left and with the plan in mind decided that it must be the cul-de-sac leading to Abbey Cottage. The Vicarage was easily located. It was a pleasant, late Georgian house approached from the road by a short drive, and separated from the church by the churchyard. The front door was standing open. In answer to Pollard's ring a stocky figure in a cassock came out of a door at the rear of the hall.

'Good morning, Sir,' Pollard said. 'You're the Reverend Martin Crabbe I take it, the Vicar of Loxford?'

'I am. And I'll hazard a guess that you're both from Scotland Yard. What can I do to help you over this shocking business? Come in.'

He led the way to his study, a good-sized room lined

125

with shelves which were packed with books. It had a large desk in the window on which were several box-files and a typewriter. There were also a number of rather shabby but comfortable-looking chairs. Martin Crabbe drew up a trio of these and invited his callers to sit down.

'I really don't think I can be of much use to you,' he said. 'I never set eyes on Miss Raymond.'

'It isn't immediately about her that we've come, Sir,' Pollard told him. 'It's to ask for your help about some enquiries we want to make in your parish. As I'm sure you've already deduced, we're here because after considering the evidence up to date our superiors at the Yard feel that Miss Raymond may have been murdered. This is by no means a certainty. One possibility is that she was shut into the feedstore as a joke, and died because she lost her head and failed to take the obvious step of switching off the car engine. A joke suggests that a child could have been responsible. Do you know of any child or group of children in your parish who might conceivably have got up to something of this sort?'

Martin Crabbe sat deep in thought for a few moments.

'No,' he said finally. 'I can't see it happening in a small, close-knit community like Loxford. And by good luck the older children are completely out of it. The over-twelves are bussed in to a comprehensive in Mallingham in term-time, and the school arranged two holiday trips for the first week in August. The older ones went to France, and the young ones to a camp twenty miles from here. I know every Loxford child went because we helped in one or two cases where money was tight. That leaves the under-twelves. Those belonging to two families are away on holiday with their parents. The rest would have been around, presumably, and of course I can't tell you what they were doing on that Wednesday morning. But I can say definitely that there's never been any trouble on Loxford House property in my time. We're not exactly feudal, but Basil Railsdon is quite somebody locally. There's another point, too. Everybody in the place knows everybody else's business, of course, and it was common knowledge that Bill Cobbledick was working on the stable block roof. I simply cannot see any local child in, say, the seven to twelve age group, risking fooling about at the feedstore with the knowledge that Bill might turn up at any moment.'

'I take it, then,' Pollard said, 'that in your opinion we can rule out any monkey tricks by the Loxford young?'

'Yes. All things considered, that's what I should do in your place.'

'Undoubtedly we shall, and we're most grateful for the way you've summed up the situation for us. You've saved us valuable time, Sir. The next thing I'd like to ask you,' Pollard went on, 'is whether there's anyone locally who is mentally abnormal and who might have shut and secured the feedstore door for a joke, knowing somebody was inside, and not, of course, realising the danger of carbon monoxide in an unventilated space?'

'We've got a feeble-minded old boy known locally as Bonky Bob, but he's pretty feeble physically, too. He spends most of his time sitting in a chair put outside his daughter's house. I don't think he could possibly have got as far as the feedstore under his own steam. Apart from him and the tragedy of a mongol child of three I think the community sanity is up to average.'

'That possible approach goes out then,' Pollard said, making a note. 'Thank you. May I ask you how long you've been in this living, Mr Crabbe?'

'Just over ten years.'

'I take it that you know the Railsdon family quite well, then, and have heard the facts about Laura Raymond's parentage?'

'Yes,' Martin Crabbe replied, 'I think I can say I do know them well, and as you've probably gathered already, my son is engaged to Mr Railsdon's daughter. It was she who told Jeremy about Laura Raymond being her father's half-sister, and he passed it on to my wife and myself. We were going up to a meal to meet her. Basil Railsdon was anxious to make her feel that she belonged to a family group. I think he felt that his father had treated her mother badly, even if he made some financial provision for her – under duress, so to speak. I mean that she could only get it under his rather inhuman conditions.'

'What I'm coming round to,' Pollard said, 'is wondering if Mr Railsdon senior had a bad reputation over women locally. Whether possibly there's someone who has a deep-seated grudge against the family, and was infuriated by Laura Raymond being recognised, so to speak.'

'It's an interesting idea,' Martin Crabbe answered. 'But I can only say that I've never heard of any local scandals about Basil's father. He seems to have gone further afield for that particular type of diversion. And you know, Chief Superintendent, if there had been talk about women in these parts I'm sure that I should have heard echoes of it. One mustn't generalise about village life, but Loxford people have amazingly long memories and old grudges seem to be handed on from one generation to the next in a family. It's usually in connection with Wills.'

'You've been most helpful, Mr Crabbe,' Pollard said as he closed his notebook, 'and I apologise for taking up your time. But before I go I must congratulate you on your son's brilliant bit of research and its outcome, and on his Research Fellowship, too, of course.'

Martin Crabbe's strong face with its matter-of-fact expression softened and lit up.

'Good show, wasn't it? He's been mad on history from his childhood. Perhaps I can claim modest credit for this, as I've always been keen on it myself, and there are plenty of books on hand.'

He indicated the well-filled shelves, adding that there were masses more around in other parts of the house.

'Is your son in at the moment?' Pollard asked. 'I want some help from him, too, and it would save time if I could have a word with him now.'

'As far as I know he's upstairs working on this book about the Overton business that a publisher has commissioned. I'll go and see.'

Left alone, Pollard reflected on the absence of any sympathetic reference to Basil Railsdon and his daughter in spite of the link established between the two families by the latter's engagement to young Crabbe. And Basil Railsdon was one of the Loxford churchwardens, too. Perhaps this had been an unavoidable appointment. There couldn't be a great many suitable candidates in a small village.

There were footsteps on the stairs and Martin Crabbe reappeared, followed by a young man in jeans and a rather tatty sweater.

'My son Jeremy, Chief Superintendent Pollard. I've told him you want a word with him. Stay and talk here. I go over to the church to read my matins about now.'

He left them together. Jeremy took the chair he had vacated and observed Pollard with speculative interest. In his turn Pollard noted the family resemblance, especially in colouring. The son had a longer and nar-

129

rower face, and looked to have rather more imagination and perception. Highly intelligent, he thought, sensing at the same time an unmistakeable caution under the surface.

'You must be cursing me,' he said, 'interrupting your work on your book. I'm completely hooked on the Aretê Overton affair, you know.'

'Are you really,' Jeremy asked with some surprise and obvious gratification. 'You know you're not a bit like what I imagined a Yard Chief Super would be.'

'Probably just as well,' Pollard replied, raising one eyebrow. 'Anyway, I respect the work you're doing far too much to take up more of your time than I need. But I'd be grateful for your detailed account of the supper party at Loxford House on the evening of Miss Raymond's arrival. By the way, I know her history and how she came to be staying there.'

Jeremy Crabbe threw himself back in his chair, clasped his hands behind his head and shut his eyes. After a few moments he opened them again and looked across at Pollard.

'The atmosphere was a bit strained,' he said. 'Laura Raymond's sudden materialisation out of the blue had given my prospective father-in-law a jolt. Understandably, to be fair. I agree that class distinctions are all wrong in theory, but I don't see how any social system can ever eliminate the cultural gap between different types of people. I couldn't care less about *who* anybody is from the family angle. But *what* he is in himself makes the hell of a lot of difference, and it's that that determines the sort of relationship that can develop between people . . . I say, am I just waffling?'

'No,' Pollard replied. 'Please carry on.'

'Well, to start with, Laura wasn't exactly easy on the eye and her clothes were appalling. She had a simply

130

hideous suburban cockney accent. But what mattered much more was her limited outlook. She was quite unable to join in general conversation on any topic that any of us could hopefully dredge up. The only thing that produced a spark of response from her was the subject of cars. She had a second-hand Mini, in Medstone, apparently. Of course all these handicaps were the outcome of the sort of life she had led as the result of being disowned by her father and left entirely to her mother, who must have been a woman of very little education or social experience. Anyway, in spite of the shock of the initial impact, Basil felt obliged to ask her down and let people know who she was, and during supper on the Tuesday night he began to realise more fully what he had let himself in for, not to mention Amanda who's engaged to me, and Henrietta Legge who's engaged to him. So it was by far the stickiest meal I've ever had to sit through. Henrietta was super. She's a marvellous person and kept things going to some extent, helped by Mandy. But I remember what a relief it was when the telephone ringing created a diversion. Basil got up and went out of the dining-room to answer it.'

'Was he out of the room long?'

'Only about a couple of minutes. He said it had been a call from Tom Whitworth who runs Loxford Farm. He's Basil's tenant, and wanted some advice about a contract he'd been offered by a canning firm, and Basil had said he'd see him at ten the next morning as the people had told Tom to phone them by noon. He – Basil, I mean – seemed a bit hipped, and told Laura he'd planned to take her for a long drive, starting at ten, and now it would have to be at half past. Laura showed some animation for the first time, and asked if it would be in the Hyperion. They'd met her at Shirbor-

131

ough station in it that afternoon. Mandy chipped in and said that Laura had fallen for the Hype. They'd had a look at it in the feedstore after tea. Then Basil said at once that he'd take her along and show her how to start it up and the gears and whatever, and she could drive it round to the front door ready to start at half past ten, and have a go on a quiet road somewhere if she felt happy with it.'

'How did she react?'

'She seemed taken aback, and said something about not knowing about that, but added that she'd like to bring it round anyway and would enjoy the drive. Was quite voluble, in fact. Well, fairly soon after that we got up from supper, and went to have coffee in the drawing-room. And at long last the party broke up. Basil took Laura off, to the feedstore presumably. Henrietta went home in her car, and Mandy and I ambled down the drive and eventually parted at the gate whence I returned here. End of chapter.'

Pollard finished some jottings in his notebook.

'Thanks for an admirably succinct and informative statement,' he said. 'And was that the last time you saw Laura Raymond?'

'Yes.'

'When did you hear about her death?'

'Mandy rang me just before lunch, when she got back from Mallingham. Rang me at Shirborough, where I was working in the Archives, not here.' Jeremy caught Pollard's eye and suddenly grinned. 'I really am in the clear, Chief Super. I went off from here in my car directly after breakfast. Say nine o'clock. Witnesses: both parents. I was in the Archives just after half past. Witness: John Grey, the County Archivist. We had a natter as soon as I got in. And I was still there when Mandy's call came through. I headed for Loxford at once, of course.'

132

'Thanks very much,' Pollard said. 'You've saved me the trouble of asking the usual routine questions. I've only one thing left to ask, in fact.'

Jeremy looked enquiring.

'Could you spare a few minutes to show me the Aretê Overton grave in the church? Wasting my time and the taxpayers' money, I admit, but I can't resist the chance of seeing it, especially with you.'

Suddenly galvanised by enthusiasm Jeremy sprang to his feet.

'What a thought,' he exclaimed. 'Let's go right now. I can hardly keep away myself.'

The church was empty, Martin Crabbe having presumably finished his devotions and departed. Pollard allowed himself a moment at the west end to take in the nave and side aisles and then followed in Jeremy's wake to the chancel. They stood side-by-side looking down.

'The gravestone broke in two when they got it up,' Jeremy said. 'No fault of Bill Cobbledick and his chaps. There was a dirty great crack running right across. He's made a good job of the replacement and repair, hasn't he?'

'Excellent,' Pollard agreed. 'The mortar's such a good match that one hardly notices the join. The sixteenth-century chap who did the lettering doesn't seem to have been very highly skilled, does he? A pretty crude effort.'

'That's right. Perhaps the nuns were hassling the poor blighter. Under the decidedly odd circumstances one can understand that they'd want to get the whole job over and done with at top speed.'

'You've probably got something there,' Pollard said, glancing round the chancel before reluctantly returning to the nave and the south door.

133

Toye was seated at the wheel of the Rover which he had parked in the road outside the entrance to the Vicarage drive and was perusing the *Daily Telegraph*.

'I just couldn't resist it,' Pollard told him, getting in after saying goodbye to Jeremy Crabbe. 'I simply had to go and take a look at the now famous non-grave. Right then. Back to Mallingham now and mulling over the next step.'

On the road Pollard passed on to Toye his impression of the Crabbes, father and son.

'Both of them,' he said, 'were carefully concealing certain feelings with a possible bearing on the case. Old Crabbe obviously takes a poor view of Railsdon, for all that he's one of the churchwardens and about to become young Jeremy's father-in-law. This may simply be a personal antipathy with no bearing on the case. Jeremy is a pleasant and very bright young man and he's worried. He was careful not to give this away by word of mouth, but I could spot the underlying tension. The moment I laid off probing and asked him to take me over to the church he was a different creature.'

'Wouldn't the fact that his girl's bound to be mixed up in all the publicity be enough to get him worried?'

'I had the feeling that his uneasiness went beyond that. However, I've no proof of this whatever, as you'll no doubt point out at any moment. Anyway, it hasn't been a wasted morning. Kids and nutcases eliminated, together with Jeremy Crabbe . . . Look, there are the towers of Mallingham Cathedral. Don't let me go inside: it would be fatal as far as getting on with the job goes.'

After some difficulty in parking they located a pleasant pub, and relaxed over a snack and the *Daily Telegraph*, Pollard annexing the crossword.

'Well,' he said later as they walked back to the car,

'my subconscious has thrown up a few ideas. So far we've adopted a – what is it called? – a centripetal approach. Approaching the nub of the problem from the outskirts. It's worked quite well so far, and I suggest that we keep on the same tack, leaving the victim's Medstone connections and the key figures, Railsdon and Miss Legge, for the moment, and side-tracking the problem of why Laura Raymond didn't switch off the Hyperion's engine and who could have banked on her not doing it.'

'Meaning we tackle Whitworth, the farmer chap, and the bloke who was hammering away on the stable roof next? Cobbledick, isn't he called? Blimey, that's an outlandish name if you like,' Toye commented.

'I don't suppose it originally meant a chap who botched his neighbours' shoe repairs. Names have got altered out of all recognition down the centuries. Like to drop into the City Library and look up "Cobble-dick"? There are some first-rate books on English surnames.'

Toye firmly vetoed this frivolous suggestion, and asked where Miss Railsdon and Mrs Bennett came in. Were they outskirts people?

'Miss Railsdon could be useful. As far as I can make out she's only been questioned about taking up the breakfast tray so far. Mrs Bennett is important, of course. She's the only person in a position to have noticed Laura Raymond's and Railsdon's movements during the critical period. Perhaps I ought to qualify that. Miss Railsdon on her own showing didn't go off in her car until just on nine-thirty. I'd much prefer to interview Mrs Bennett in her employer's absence. A man like Railsdon must have quite a lot of outside commitments, and the person likely to know about them is Miss Legge. It's important to interview Miss Legge on

135

her home ground and not at Loxford House with Railsdon hovering about. I'm thinking of ringing her tonight and asking for an appointment early tomorrow morning. How does all this strike you?'

After consideration Toye agreed that it looked to him a good working basis.

'Let's push on, then,' Pollard said as they arrived at the car park.

Abbey Farm was on the Mallingham side of Loxford House and was approached by a track running north from the main road, between wire fences. Pollard, who had a brother who farmed in Sussex, eyed the land on each side critically. It looked well-tended and prosperous. The farmhouse and buildings were in good shape. As they drew up a middle-aged man in shirtsleeves appeared in the yard and came towards them enquiringly.

'Mr Whitworth?' Pollard asked, holding out his official card. 'Chief Superintendent Pollard and Inspector Toye of Scotland Yard. We are hoping you may be able to help us over one or two points in the enquiry into the late Miss Raymond's death.'

Tom Whitworth inevitably replied that he had already told the Inspector from Shirborough everything he could, and that wasn't much, but if they liked to come into the office and take a seat, fair enough. He led the way to a small, single-storey building fitted up with a desk, files, shelves bearing an assortment of pamphlets and reference books, a typewriter and sundry other pieces of office equipment. He indicated a couple of upright wooden chairs and took another himself.

'Farming in the eighties?' Pollard commented, indicating the surroundings.

'That's right. You need to be twenty-five per cent

136

business man these days. That's where I'm lucky to have a landlord like Mr Railsdon. Sees his way through a maze of figures quick as lightning and what's going to pay off best. Never grudges his time to help you, neither. He'll make us a first-rate M.P.'

Pollard took up the opening.

'It was something to do with plans for the farm you went over to Loxford House to see him about last Wednesday morning, wasn't it?'

'That's right. We've got quite a bit of land down to soft fruit, and the cannery wants us to step up production. I wasn't sure how it would work out, what with the initial cost of the change-over, even with better terms from the cannery. They want to expand production themselves, see? They'd got a board meeting coming up, and wanted figures.'

'When you went over to see Mr Railsdon he was in, waiting for you, wasn't he?'

'Yes, he was coming out of his study as I came to the front door. The grandfather in the hall was striking the hour.'

'Now, Mr Whitmore, this is important. While you were with Mr Railsdon did you hear anyone coming down the stairs and going across the hall to the front door. Please think very carefully.'

Tom Whitworth sat with his hands on his knees, a frown on his weatherbeaten face, staring at the wall behind Pollard's head.

'I couldn't say more than I heard somebody about in the house, but 'twether whoever 'twas came down the stairs or was goin' up 'em, that I can't say. Back of my mind I thought Emily Bennett was around, but not to put it into words to myself, if you get me. And Bill Cobbledick was makin' a row up on the stable block roof.'

'And you and Mr Railsdon were alone together in the study all the time from when you arrived until Miss Legge arrived?'

'That's right. Both of us together, first to last. I knew he wanted to get off at half past ten, and was just gettin' up when we heard somebody runnin' and the door burst open. White as a sheet, poor Miss Legge was, but not hysterical-like. She's not that sort.'

'How long did it take you and Mr Railsdon to get to the feedstore?'

'Not much over a minute, I'd say. We fair ran hell for leather.'

'You didn't see anybody around as you arrived?'

'Not a soul. We got the poor lady out and laid her on the grass. Miss Legge had come along afterwards, and Mr Railsdon asked her to go and dial 999 for an ambulance. Then he ripped off his coat and started artificial respiration. When he was nearly flat out and I took over he went to holler to Bill Cobbledick to come down off the roof and take a turn. We put all we'd got into it but 'tweren't no manner of use.'

'What's your opinion of the cause of Miss Raymond not being able to get out of the feedstore, Mr Whitworth?' Pollard asked.

The farmer scowled deeply and scratched his head.

'It's the queerest thing that's ever come my way. I reckon she wasn't used to cars in the Hyperion class, and maybe she made a muck of startin' 'er up, and lost grip, like. As to somebody fastening the door, well there's nobody in Loxford who'd do a thing like that. There's no maniacs around here.'

'You know that Miss Raymond was Mr Railsdon's illegitimate half-sister?'

'Everyone in the place knows it now, and that Mr Railsdon didn't know she existed till early this summer.

138

And 'tis felt he acted very proper in having 'er down right away, as one of the family, for all that she was wrong side o' the blanket.'

Asked if Mr Railsdon's father had had a bad reputation locally over women, Tom Whitworth replied that he'd never heard so, but he himself wasn't a native of Loxford. Feeling that there was little more to be gained by further questioning Pollard thanked Tom Whitworth for his cooperation and began to bring the interview to a close. Remarking that he must go along to Loxford House he learnt that Basil Railsdon had gone up to London for the day. Emily Bennett would be around, and maybe Miss Amanda if she wasn't off with her young man.

'I want a look at the feedstore and the general lie of the land,' Pollard said. 'And also to contact Mr Cobbledick. Perhaps you'd tell me where he lives.'

'You won't find him at his own place, not in working hours. Reckon you'd do better to go along after five when he'll've knocked off and got back. On the right as you make for Shirborough, near the far end of the village. There's a board up. You can't miss it . . . Don't think the worse of him if he's a bit short. He's not got over his little grandchild's disappearin' a couple of months back. Better than he was, and was down at the pub last night, but not 'is old self yet.'

Prompted by Toye, Pollard, who had been preoccupied with a case in the north at the time, recollected the tragedy.

'Poor chap,' he said. 'Thanks for mentioning it to us. We'll bear it in mind.'

Leaving the farm they returned to the main road, and shortly afterwards turned into the Loxford House drive.

'Pull up a minute,' Pollard told Toye. 'Let's get the hang of the place.'

139

It was, he thought, a most attractive set up. On the right of the drive a belt of trees separated the grounds from the fields of Abbey Farm. On its left, the lower part of the land sloping gently up to the house had been planted as a glade of magnolias, azaleas and rhododendrons. The flowering season was virtually over, but it must be a blaze of colour in late spring and early summer. North of this and in front of the house was a lawn with flower-beds and a couple of magnificent copper beeches. On the north side of the house was another area of grass and trees, and a small area of woodland extended up the hillside to the north-east. From the point where the car had come to a halt it was just possible to see a small one-storey building in front of the trees, presumably the feedstore.

Loxford House itself had apparently been rebuilt in the eighteenth century. It was two-storeyed with well-spaced windows in the west-facing façade, and a handsome front door surmounted by a pediment. An extension had been built out at the back, at the south-east corner. The whole exterior gave the impression of having been recently redecorated, and the house was fresh and white against its background of trees. Toye commented that whatever might be wrong there was no shortage of cash up there.

Pollard gave a grunt of assent, and sat on in silence staring at Loxford House. Was money, he thought, at the root of this exceedingly odd case? If so, and Laura Raymond was attempting to blackmail Railsdon, she must have been in a position of considerable strength for him to have even considered her murder. And so far there had not been a whisper of scandal involving the chap. As to old Railsdon, well, these days people didn't pay all that much attention to the sins of the

140

fathers . . . Following up the blackmail idea, had Henrietta Legge seen a threat to the life of security and affluence that she had been looking forward to as Railsdon's wife? In theory, of course, the location of Abbey Cottage made it possible for her to have done the whole job herself, and she was at supper on the Tuesday evening when the plan for Laura Raymond to bring the Hyperion round to the house was discussed. On the other hand she, too, seemed to have an impeccable local reputation.

Pollard's thoughts moved to Laura Raymond herself. Experience had taught him that the detection of a killer was sometimes achieved through a thorough investigation into the victim's character and past life. A visit to Medstone was unavoidable. The local C.I.D. had unearthed the basic facts about her but it would be necessary to probe more deeply from the look of things, especially about her mental state. Was she liable to hysteria or brainstorms?

'Railsdon's being away for the day is the pointer to our next move,' he said, surfacing. 'Young Amanda may be at home, and if so, we'll have a chat with her. More about her reactions to Raymond and her visit than her own doings that Wednesday morning. We've the evidence of the driver of the mail van that she was outward-bound in her car just before nine-thirty, and she didn't reappear until Sergeant Jones was on the point of leaving. Shirborough have checked with her hairdresser in Mallingham. If she's off somewhere with Jeremy Crabbe or elsewhere we'll concentrate on Mrs Bennett, and then inspect the lie of the land.'

Mrs Emily Bennett was small, spectacled and grey-haired, neatly dressed in a long-sleeved frock. Pollard noted that the eyes behind the spectacles were shrewd. He introduced himself and Toye and proffered his official card. She barely glanced at it, and informed him that Mr Railsdon had gone up to London for the day for a board meeting and would not be back until seven o'clock at the earliest. He had told her to show Superintendent Pollard from Scotland Yard any part of the house and grounds he wanted to see. Having delivered this message she stood waiting expectantly on the threshold.

'That was very helpful of him,' Pollard said. 'We should like to have a look at the room Miss Raymond had, to start with.'

Mrs Bennett led the way up a wide staircase to the first-floor landing, and turned to the left. Amanda's bedroom occupied the south-west corner of the building, and Laura Raymond's was immediately beyond it, near the beginning of the easterly extension of the house which Pollard had noticed. Further on again was a bathroom, and facing its door a minor staircase leading down to the ground floor. Mrs Bennett informed them that it led to the kitchen quarters.

'Then Miss Raymond could have gone down this way and out into the grounds without going through the hall?' Pollard asked.

Mrs Bennett agreed. The back door was at the end of the passage immediately below the one where they were standing, and she kept it open most of the time in summer. It led into the stable yard.

'I'd have seen her for sure if I'd been in the kitchen,' she added, 'but I was coming and going to the dining-room as I've said before.'

Laura Raymond's room had been searched by the two constables deputed to do it by Inspector Blair, and he had mentioned in his report that nothing relevant to the enquiry had been found. Mrs Bennett added the information that Mr Railsdon had said nothing was to

142

be touched or removed, and that the room had not even been cleaned, a matter which clearly rankled with her. Pollard and Toye quickly investigated drawers and cupboards and the suitcase on a luggage stand. At the back of a drawer was a plastic handbag containing a cheque book, a notecase with twenty pounds in notes, a purse containing loose change and a return ticket from Shirborough to London. The suitcase was unlocked and empty. The pockets of clothes hanging in the wardrobe were empty, and under the pillows there was merely a neatly-folded nightdress.

At Pollard's suggestion they went down the staircase opposite the bathroom, and walked along the passage past the kitchen to the open back door. Here he and Toye studied the stable yard and the newly-roofed garages on the far side. Mrs Bennett confirmed that the track coming through the trees on the left led to the feedstore.

'That's all quite clear, thank you,' Pollard said. 'Could we sit down somewhere for a few minutes now and check up on one or two points?'

'Mr Railsdon said to use the dining-room as being convenient if you wanted to talk to me. It's this way, if you please.'

He did not miss the note of controlled exasperation in her voice as she led the way towards the front of the house and into a panelled room to the left of the front door, and as they sat down at a fine refectory table he decided on his approach.

'We haven't come to pester you with questions about whether you heard anyone coming downstairs on the day of Miss Raymond's death, and if you did, when,' he told her. 'Obviously it's quite impossible for you to be definite about it. But there is a way in which you might be able to help us quite a lot. One of the difficulties fac-

143

ing us is that she was a stranger to all intents and purposes. Mr Railsdon had met her once in London. Miss Railsdon, Miss Legge, Mr Jeremy Crabbe and yourself had never seen her before the Tuesday of last week. Of course we shall make enquiries about her at Medstone where she lived, but at the moment we're working on the situation that developed down here. Now, you have been a member of this household for a good many years, and must have seen a large number of visitors come and go and sized them up. An opinion from somebody like you is worth having. What did you make of Miss Raymond? Anything you say will be treated in confidence unless – and it's most unlikely – it has to come out as evidence in court.'

Mrs Bennett gave him a keen glance, appeared to debate within herself, and finally clasped her hands together and rested them on the table.

'I wouldn't discuss Mr Railsdon's guests with anybody, not in the ordinary way,' she said, 'but things having turned out the way they have I can't see I'm being disloyal to him, and if you think it might help you to get this nasty business cleared up, well, fair enough. Mr Railsdon came out to my sitting-room one evening and told me the whole story: that she was his illegitimate half-sister that he knew nothing about, and how she'd only just found out that they'd had the same father. She'd written to him, his lawyer in London had gone into it and found it was quite true. She'd had a rough time, and he'd gone up to London to meet her, and he felt he wanted to make it up to her by asking her down here as one of the family . . . Well,' Mrs Bennett raised her clasped hands and let them fall back on to the table, 'when she turned up and Miss Amanda brought her out to the kitchen to see me you could've knocked me down with a feather.'

144

'What surprised you so much, Mrs Bennett?' Pollard asked.

'Why, that he'd brought a person like her down here to be on a level with Miss Amanda and Miss Legge who's going to be his wife, and expecting all his friends to treat her like one of themselves. Common as dirt, she was, the way she spoke and the things she said and her loud, common clothes. Not a manner to her. I was in and out of the dining-room during supper that Tuesday night, and heard her speaking plain rude. You could see that she'd never mixed with gentry in her life. Maybe that was no fault of hers, but as I see it Mr Railsdon should never have forced her on to Miss Amanda and Miss Legge as he did. I've always worked for gentry and I know their ways. And if she'd been visiting here once she'd expect to come again. Expect to come to our two weddings, I don't doubt. People wouldn't have known where to look.'

'Don't you think it was a generous thing for Mr Railsdon to do?' Pollard suggested. 'After all, they'd had the same father, and she'd been disowned and missed out on a very great deal.'

'It could never have made for her own happiness in the long run,' Mrs Bennett asserted doggedly. 'That I'm sure of. She'd never have fitted in. Chalk won't mix with cheese. I can't understand why Mr Railsdon couldn't see it from the start. He's clear-headed enough as a rule. I keep on puzzling over it.'

'What did Miss Railsdon and Miss Legge feel about it all?'

'I can't say what Miss Legge felt. I don't know her well enough as yet. But it was plain to see that she was doing her best to smooth things over. She would, being the lady she is from a real Crantshire county family. As to Miss Amanda, well, she was sorry for Miss Raymond

145

and showed it. She's got what you'd call a sympathetic nature and seems to know what other folk feel, but you could see she was finding it hard going, bless her. Took up Miss Raymond's breakfast tray the next morning, knowing what I felt about waiting on the likes of her.'

'I take it Miss Railsdon's out?' Pollard asked.

'That's right. Out with young Mr Crabbe. They go out together afternoons and he works at the book he's writing mornings and evenings. They're getting married on the sixteenth of December. Proper pair of lovebirds,' Mrs Bennett added, mellowing perceptibly.

'Right up your street,' Pollard remarked, turning to Toye. 'Inspector Toye's a romantic at heart, Mrs Bennett, although he looks such a serious type.'

Toye, adept at picking up a lead, observed that it looked like being a popular match in Loxford with both the young people being local. Mrs Bennett gave him an approving glance, and replied that what with Mr Railsdon's marrying Miss Legge, and then Miss Amanda and Mr Crabbe's wedding in December, the Ring of Bells would do well with all the drinking of healths.'

'Mind you,' she said, 'Mr Railsdon wasn't keen on the match, not to start with. He was aiming a bit higher for Miss Amanda. A title maybe. Not that he could stop them: they're both of age. But what with Mr Jeremy making quite a name for himself over that grave down at the church and getting a post at an Oxford College he came right round a month or so back.'

'Well,' Pollard said, 'we've had an interesting talk, Mrs Bennett, and many thanks for all your help. We shall want a word with Miss Amanda, and to see Mr Railsdon about one or two points. Possibly tomorrow morning. I'll be ringing him. And before we take ourselves off we want to have a good look at the feedstore. Don't bother to take us along. We saw the track starting off from the stable yard, you remember.'

Once they were out of earshot Toye expressed himself forcibly on the subject of Mrs Bennett's class-consciousness.

'And who's she herself?' he demanded rhetorically. 'Made me see red, she did.'

'Small or capital R?' Pollard asked with amusement. 'All right, old man, I'm only pulling your leg. She's a variation on the Faithful Retainer theme: the type that identifies with its employers. It says in the file that she was on the staff of Ollsford Castle down in the south of Crantshire, where her husband was a gardener, and so she's been breathing socially rarefied air all her working life. But to keep what passes for our minds on the job – Mrs Bennett's reaction to Laura Raymond seems to support the idea that Railsdon could have been blackmailed into asking her down on a visit. Do you agree?'

'Yes,' Toye replied unequivocally. 'All the guff about making up to Raymond for all she'd been done out of by old Railsdon doesn't seem to tie in with wanting his girl to marry somebody with a title, to start with.'

'No, it doesn't,' Pollard said thoughtfully. 'I thought Bennett's remark about Railsdon being clear-headed was interesting, too. And Whitworth said much the same thing in a different way. We'll form our own opinion of him tomorrow.'

The track leading to the feedstore passed among trees whose fresh green of early summer had passed into the darker, drooping heaviness of August. The general effect was gloomy and oddly depressing, Pollard thought. In less than a minute the solid, uncompromising cube of the feedstore loomed up. They walked round it, inspecting the outside. The door was wide open, propped by a stone, and to Toye's keen disappointment there was no car inside.

'I expect Railsdon drove himself into Shirborough and went up to Town by train,' Pollard commented. 'Board meetings usually start fairly early.' He walked in and looked round the starkly empty interior. Apart from dust, dead leaves and some fragments of string and paper it was wholly uninformative. The two gratings that he had observed in the side walls were, as Inspector Blair had noted, blocked by rust and dirt and thickly encrusted with spiders' webs containing vestiges of dead flies. He prodded vigorously and shook them, but found them immoveable, and was satisfied that they had not been shifted since they were put in when the feedstore was being built.

'This is where we go over that stile and across the meadow to Miss Legge's cottage,' he said. 'Timing ourselves, and hoping she isn't looking out of a back window. It's that pink cottage, for sure. I don't want to get involved with her, until we've interviewed all the bit part people.'

There was a very faint track from the stile to the gate on the far side. They followed it, eyes on the ground from sheer force of habit, though as Pollard remarked, what they expected to find was anyone's guess. The meadow had been cut for hay and the crop carried, but there was no sign of litter, suggesting, as Toye pointed out, that the track was not considered a public footpath and anyway it only led slap bang into the middle of Railsdon's property.

'Under four minutes,' Pollard said, looking at his watch as they arrived at the gate. It was a rather ancient five-bar wooden gate secured, like the feedstore, with a staple and hasp. Toye opened it and they slipped through quietly, taking cover by the hedge on their right. Beyond this was a small vegetable garden belonging to Abbey Cottage, and they had a view of the back of the building. The windows shone with cleanliness and the curtains were fresh-looking and carefully hung, but it was obvious that the exterior needed repointing and that a new roof would be a sound investment in the near future. A cottage of much the same type on the opposite side of the lane was in a poor state of repair and up for sale. Telling Toye to stay put, Pollard moved to a position from which he could see the front of Abbey Cottage. It gave the same impression as the back. There was an attractive flower garden and a small wooden garage. This was open and empty, and the sound of a car driving rather slowly along the village street sent him swiftly to cover beside Toye. It proved a false alarm however, and they began to retrace their steps across the meadow at what they felt was a reasonable pace for a young woman of thirty who was not in any particular hurry.

'Four minutes plus,' Pollard said as they arrived at the stile. 'Uphill in this direction. The times tie in with Miss Legge's statement. She was washing her hands at about ten-twenty, she said, and then started out. Say she got here just after half past. According to Whitworth as well as Railsdon and Mrs Bennett, she burst into the house at twenty to eleven approx. That would be about right for the time taken in opening the feed-store, switching off the Hyperion's engine and dashing over to the house. Another bit of confirmation is that she obviously is, or has been, hard-up. You've only got to look at the outside of that cottage. So we haven't altogether wasted our time. It's only a quarter past four though. Too early to descend on Cobbledick. So what?'

Toye remarked that a cuppa wouldn't come amiss as

far as he was concerned, and that there had been a notice on the Mallingham road saying FARMHOUSE TEAS ¼ MILE.

'Lead me to it,' Pollard replied.

Twenty minutes later they were seated at a trestle table on a shaggy lawn in front of a farmhouse very similar to Tom Whitworth's, although slightly less prosperous-looking. The farmer's wife, unexpectedly young and with-it, brought out homemade scones and jam and a generous basin of clotted cream, together with a large teapot. She told them to come and give a shout at the kitchen door round at the back if they wanted more hot water, and left them to it. There were no other patrons, and they ate and drank in relaxed contentment, contemplating the great sweep of rural landscape spread out before them. Finally Pollard looked at his watch.

'Half past five. O.K. for the Cobbledick call by the time we get there.'

He went round to the kitchen door, to the disapproval of a gaggle of purposeful-looking farm dogs whose challenge brought the farmer's wife to the door. As the uproar subsided Pollard paid the bill, congratulated her on her cooking and went to rejoin Toye in the Rover.

'Any special line with Cobbledick?' Toye asked, as they drove.

'Only that we go easy, as recommended by Whitworth. Poor devil, even if he was only the kid's grandfather. These cases of small children vanishing into thin air and leaving a lifetime of hideous speculations behind simply gets me down . . . I don't think Cobbledick's likely to be much direct use, but any line on Railsdon and Miss Legge could be useful.'

They had no difficulty in finding the house from Tom

Whitworth's directions. The door was opened by a man in the later fifties at Pollard's estimate, weatherbeaten and with a dogged expression.

'Mr Cobbledick?' Pollard held out his official card and introduced Toye and himself. 'If you're free, we'd like to find out if you can give us any help over this enquiry we've been sent down here to carry out.'

'I'm free till choir practice at eight. Come inside if you want to, but the Shirborough chaps have had the little I know twice over.'

'Thank you,' Pollard said, following him down a flagged passage to a large kitchen-cum-living-room where a faded little woman was stacking a dishwasher.'

'Scotland Yard, Mother,' Bill announced briefly. 'Come about Mr Railsdon's sister. My wife, gentlemen.'

Mrs Cobbledick, who had swung round, burst into tears.

'Oh God!' she sobbed. 'Just for a minute I thought – I thought . . .'

Unable to control herself, she ran from the room.

'Best to let her be,' Bill said heavily. 'She took it you'd come about our little grandchild. Maybe you haven't heard the story.'

Pollard assured him that they had.

'As coppers we come up against some horrific things,' he said, 'but do believe me we're appalled about this particular tragedy, and that you've got our very real sympathy. And we hate bothering you about this other disaster.'

'Reckon life's got to go on. Sit round the table, shall us?'

Chairs were indicated. As Pollard sat down he brought into play his ability to absorb his surroundings in a matter of seconds. Originally a farmhouse kitchen,

151

he thought, registering dark oak beams, whitewashed walls and stone flags under strips of carpet and matting. The former open hearth was now occupied by an Aga and a small electric cooker. As well as the dishwasher there was an electric mixer on a side table, and he could see a washing machine through a half-open door. There were radiators, a colour television set and a cassette recorder, and comfortable armchairs at the end of the room which housed the table round which they were sitting. Doing pretty well, he reflected, and rather unexpectedly finding an outlet in music.

'We don't want to waste your time, Mr Cobbledick,' he began, 'so let's go straight in, shall we? I take it you know that the late Miss Raymond was an illegitimate half-sister of Mr Railsdon?'

'I do. All Loxford knows b'now. He made no secret of it before she came down on a visit.'

'Did you know she was arriving on Tuesday of last week?'

'No, I didn't. 'Twas all round the village that he'd sent her an invite, but not for when.'

'So you hadn't seen her before Mr Railsdon called you to come and lend a hand with the artificial respiration?'

'That's right. When he came hollerin' that there'd been an accident in the feedstore I was afraid it could be Miss Amanda or Miss Legge, and I came down off the stable roof like lightning. But while I was runnin' I remembered hearin' Miss Amanda goin' off in her car about half past nine. I couldn't think who 'twas when I got there, till he told me to take me coat off and take a turn to see if we could bring his sister round.'

'You'd been to the feedstore earlier on, hadn't you?' Pollard asked.

'Correct. I started work eight o'clock, same as usual,

and went in to get the weathercock Mr Railsdon'd bought to go up on the stable block. Nice bit o' metalwork it is, and I'd left it where he put it when he brought it back in his car. The door was fastened, and everythin' inside same as always, with the Hyperion takin' up most o' the place. I got the weathercock an' came out an' fastened the door, and I'll say so on the Bible oath if need be.'

There was a short pause.

'I know you can't see the feedstore even from the ridge of the stable block roof,' Pollard said. 'Inspector Blair told me he'd been up there himself. But did you by chance see anybody about in any other part of the grounds that morning? Before you were called down by Mr Railsdon, I mean?'

'Couldn't have. I was finishin' the last bit of the roof, on the far side. All you can see from that side's the woods up the slope and the downs up top, and anyway I'd got my back to 'em. I came down for the last lot o' pantiles, but I'd stacked 'em ready at the bottom o' the ladder and didn't go round to the front.'

Pollard decided on a circuitous approach to Bill Cobbledick's opinion of Basil Railsdon.

'Well,' he said, 'thank you for confirming all your previous statements so definitely. And that's all, really, except that Inspector Toye and I feel you've made a simply first-rate job of that roof. We took time off to admire it this afternoon.'

Toye added his opinion that the pantiles were fine, and looked just the ticket.

Bill Cobbledick, obviously gratified, admitted that they were the real thing. Mr Railsdon was a dab at spotting what was going, and had noticed them on an old barn that was being taken down. No synthetic modern stuff for him, not on his place. Why, bits of it went back to the sixteen hundreds.

'Nice to work for a chap like that,' Pollard commented.

'He's particular an' you've got to go his way, but he knows good work when he sees it, an' pays on the nail.'

No further views appeared to be forthcoming, so after expressing his regret at having distressed Mrs Cobbledick Pollard got up to leave.

'A certain lack of enthusiasm about Railsdon, didn't you think?' he asked as they drove away. 'Rather different from Whitworth's attitude.'

'Could be that he lets Whitworth feel a bit more of a partner, seeing that the farm's part of the Loxford House estate and it's imporant for his own standing that it's a success,' Toye suggested.

'You may have got something there . . . Do you know, on second thoughts I'm not going to ring Miss Legge about tomorrow morning. She'll almost certainly get in touch with Railsdon later tonight if I do. Of course she must know that we'll turn up sooner or later, but in the interests of the enquiry it'll pay better to catch her on the hop. We'll turn up early, though.'

Chapter Seven

According to plan, Pollard and Toye breakfasted early the following morning, and called in at the Shirborough police headquarters by eight-thirty. They did not expect any fresh information to have come in and none awaited them, but Pollard always made a point of keeping the local C.I.D. briefed. Inspector Blair was appreciative and inclined to the theory of collaboration between Basil Railsdon and Henrietta Legge.

'We're off now to catch the lady before she goes over to Loxford House,' Pollard told him. 'From what Mrs Bennett said, Railsdon doesn't come down to breakfast until after nine, and retires to his study with his mail as soon as it comes at nine-thirty approx.'

It had rained overnight and the morning was fresh and sunny with white cumulus clouds bowling across a clear blue sky. Pollard allowed himself to feel reasonably satisfied with the progress made so far. Toye kept up a good speed and the tower of Loxford church came in sight at twenty minutes past nine. He slowed for the left turn into the cul-de-sac and drew up sharply. A large opulent car which he instantly identified as a Jaguar XJ12 was drawn up outside Abbey Cottage.

'Damn,' Pollard said. 'Anyway, it's not the Hyper-

155

ion, and I can't believe a Mallingham garage would have a car in that class on hire. And it's got a Surrey number. Find somewhere to park along the road and we'll walk up.'

As they approached Abbey Cottage on foot they saw that the front door was open. Voices were audible. In response to a nod Toye rang the bell vigorously. A door on the left opened and a youngish woman came out quickly, closing it behind her. She was a little above average height, slim and dark-haired with well-cut features, deep blue eyes, and was obviously in a state of some tension, barely waiting for Pollard to introduce Toye and himself.

'Good morning,' she said rather breathlessly. 'I knew you would come sooner or later, of course, but look, can you help me get rid of these people inside? They want to buy this cottage and obviously don't mind what they pay, but it simply isn't for sale.'

They exchanged glances of mutual comprehension, Pollard alive to Toye's disapproval of this unorthodox opening of the interrogation of a suspect.

'I'll certainly have a go, Miss Legge,' he told her. 'May we come in?'

He followed her into an attractive cottage sitting-room, much larger than he had expected. It had a low ceiling, and a big open fireplace, flanked by alcoves containing obviously good china. A couple seated side-by-side on a sofa radiated a degree of affluence commensurate with the car in the lane. The man sketched a gesture of getting to his feet. Henrietta introduced them to Pollard as Mr and Mrs Tremlett-Brown. He placed them as a prosperous businessman and his wife looking round for a congenial retirement home. Mr Tremlett-Brown was solid, sleek and assured. His wife, who had probably started off as a fluffy blonde, had also put on

156

weight. She was conventionally but expensively dressed, and her jewellery and make-up were marginally excessive. On hearing who the new arrivals were they both appeared taken aback and distinctly annoyed.

Pollard sat down in an armchair by Henrietta's, facing the sofa. Toye had muttered something about making more room and disappeared, leaving the door fractionally ajar.

'I'm sorry to have interrupted your call on Miss Legge,' he said, 'but I'm conducting some enquiries on behalf of the police and am afraid they must take precedence.'

Mr Tremlett-Brown's jaw became more set.

'If Miss Legge will undertake to consider the offer I've just made for this place and contact me before tonight at the Imperial Hotel, Shirborough, we'll clear off right away,' he replied impassively.

'But it's already sold, isn't it, Miss Legge?' Pollard asked, a faint note of surprise in his voice. 'Hasn't Mr Railsdon of Loxford House bought it and is having the deeds transferred to his daughter as a wedding present?'

'Yes, he has,' Henrietta replied briefly. 'So there is really no point in discussing the matter any further, Mr Tremlett-Brown.'

Mrs Tremlett-Brown instantly became a woman convinced of her personal charm and its efficacy in wearing down opposition. Henrietta and Pollard were treated to a display of archly raised eyebrows, tilted head, appealing glances at themselves and the ceiling, and little fluttering movements of her hands.

'Dear Miss Legge, you can't be so cruel! We've absolutely fallen flat for this lovely cottage, haven't we, Josh? It is what we've always hoped to find for our "eventide" home. We both feel we were *guided* to come and look for it in this part of the country.'

157

They sat looking at her with detached interest but refrained from making the expected comment that the search was surely premature. After a perceptible pause she went on to explain that they were devoting a fortnight's holiday to the quest.

'We came down last Monday week, didn't we, Josh, and started off by going to Ling and Grant in Shirborough. They're easily the best estate agents in these parts, aren't they? Some friends of ours got an absolute gem of a house in the New Forest through them. They were most helpful, and we came away with a whole bunch of particulars about suitable properties and where to get the keys. We sorted them into the different areas and came over this way to look at about half-a-dozen last Wednesday. Or was it Thursday, Josh?'

'Wednesday,' he replied categorically. 'We did the ones west of Shirborough on Tuesday, and the coastal lot on Thursday.'

'So we did! A week ago today. How time flies, doesn't it? We walked up the lane as it looked a bit narrow for parking, and before we got to Pilgrim Cottage over the way – well, we caught sight of this one. And of you, through one of the bedroom windows, busy hoovering! You could hear it,' Mrs Tremlett-Brown concluded with a little moue at Henrietta.

Mr Tremlett-Brown abruptly took over.

'Having come all this way we spent a good bit of time in the other cottage to see if it would modernise and enlarge into the sort of place we want. The only satisfactory way of building out would be at the back. Who owns that field behind it?'

'Mr Railsdon of Loxford House,' Henrietta replied. 'Actually he and I are getting married early next month, and I feel sure that he wouldn't consider selling any of the meadow.'

158

The Tremlett-Browns looked staggered, and a twitter of excited interest from Mrs Tremlett-Brown rapidly changed to a pathetic little wail.

'And to think of all the time we spent here last Wednesday morning, working out how we could enlarge that cottage over there by building out at the back. And then I wanted to come across here and find out if you'd consider selling this one if we made it really worth your while. I wanted to, but I'm the impulsive one and Josh said we'd better look at all the others Ling and Grant had given us first.'

Pollard registered a small abrupt movement by Henrietta. Obviously she had realised the possible implications of the Tremlett-Brown presence on that morning.

'I think I must come in on this,' he said. 'As you are strangers to this part of the country you probably don't know that my colleague and I are here to enquire into an unexplained death in the building on the far side of the meadow behind these cottages last Wednesday morning, at some time between roughly nine-fifteen and ten-thirty. We are interested in anyone noticed in that meadow or near that building during that period.'

Mr Tremlett-Brown looked interested, dropped his aggressive attitude over the possible purchase of Abbey Cottage or part of the meadow, and became the experienced businessman with the capacity to grasp a situation.

'I reckon what you want to know is just when we were here that morning, and what we saw or didn't see?'

'Exactly,' Pollard replied. 'This information could be very valuable,' he added, taking out a notebook, although well aware that Toye would be recording the conversation outside the door.

The Tremlett-Browns had made an early start from

their hotel in Shirborough, having a busy day's house-hunting ahead of them. They had parked in the main street, collected the keys of the cottage they were going to view from the post office, and reached it just after twenty-five minutes past nine. Abbey Cottage caught their eye as they walked up the cul-de-sac, and they had paused to admire it, also getting a glimpse of Miss Legge who could be heard hoovering an upstairs room. They had then inspected the exterior of the cottage that they had come to see before going inside for a critical look round. They agreed almost at once that the place had possibilities but would need enlarging by being built out at the back, and went to an upstairs back window to see what lay beyond the hedge at the rear of the property.

'What time would it have been when you were looking at the meadow from this window?' Pollard asked.

They agreed together that a quarter to ten would be near enough.

'I want you both to think carefully before you answer my next question. Try to picture the meadow as you stood looking at it . . . Right? Now, what do you remember thinking about it?'

They had both thought it a good size, and sloping gently upwards towards a small wood. It had been cut for hay. No animals were grazing it, and there was no sign of anybody about. On the far side they had noticed a building looking like a shed for storage, up near the trees. It had a big black door.

'Was this door open or shut?' Pollard asked, trying to keep any suggestion of undue interest out of his voice.

Both were emphatic that the door was wide open, that there was something inside the building that might have been a farm cart, but it was too far away to be sure. They were, of course, mainly interested in the

160

lower part of the meadow just over the hedge, and agreed that if they offered a good price it ought not to be difficult to persuade the owner to sell enough to make it possible to enlarge the cottage and make a good-sized vegetable garden. Then they had come downstairs again, and sat on a seat outside the front door talking things over. By this time it must have been nearly ten o'clock. As they were sitting there, they had seen Miss Legge cutting flowers in her garden, and Mrs Tremlett-Brown had suggested calling to ask her if she would consider selling her cottage, and if not, whether she could tell them who owned the meadow. Mr Tremlett-Brown had been against this idea, maintaining that the proper way to set about making an offer would be through Ling and Grant. In the end his wife had given in. They had locked up, gone out into the lane and walked as far as the gate into the meadow to have another look at the section they might want to buy.

'Nobody in sight this time, either,' Mr Tremlett-Brown concluded. 'Pam'll bear me out. But somebody'd shut the door of that shed affair while we'd been sitting in the garden.'

'That's right,' she concurred. 'And it was ten past ten when we came away. I remember looking at my watch and saying we'd better get a move on.'

'Would you both,' Pollard asked, 'be prepared to repeat what you've just told me in court if it became necessary?'

Mrs Tremlett-Brown cast up her eyes and made a despairing gesture, but clearly found the prospect acceptable.

'Certainly we should,' her husband said irritably. 'It's people's duty to cooperate with the police. Here's our address and telephone number if you want to contact

161

us,' he added, taking a card from his wallet and handing it to Pollard. 'And if that's all, we'll be off. Good morning to you,' he added getting to his feet.

'Good morning, and thank you for your help,' Pollard replied, rising to shake the hand extended by Mrs Tremlett-Brown.

Henrietta escorted the couple to the front door, and stood waiting politely on the step until the garden gate closed behind them. She returned to the sitting-room looking composed, if pale, and invited Pollard to sit down again. Toye slipped in unobtrusively and occupied a seat in the corner.

'I'm sorry you've had this hold-up, Chief Superintendent,' she said.

'On the contrary, Miss Legge,' he told her, 'Mr and Mrs Tremlett-Brown have saved me a lot of time. You see, I have to ask everyone who had any contact with Miss Raymond about his or her movements last Wednesday morning, haven't I, and as far as yours are concerned they've pretty well covered the ground for me.'

He spoke pleasantly and she gave him a small, tremulous smile. Her mouth was one of her most attractive features, he thought. Too wide on strictly aesthetic grounds but sensitive and expressive.

'I understand that, of course,' she said. 'Please don't think I resent it, only – only it's a bit shattering suddenly finding oneself considered as a potential murderer. I suppose' – she broke off and passed the back of her hand across her forehead – 'that although it seems clear now that I couldn't have shut the door of the feed-store, there's only my word for it that I found it wasn't fastened when I was going past at about half past ten. I mean, it could be thought that I was sheltering someone else couldn't it?'

'It could,' Pollard replied, 'but I haven't come along

162

this morning to follow up that possibility, but to talk to you about Miss Raymond herself and her visit here. When did you first hear of her existence, and that she'd been invited to Loxford House?'

Watching Henrietta Legge closely he saw that she was surprised rather than relieved. She was silent for a moment, briefly shutting her eyes as if collecting her thoughts.

'I suppose you know all about her letter to my future husband claiming the half-sister relationship?' she asked.

'Yes, we do. Inspector Blair has passed on her original letter to him, a carbon copy of his reply to it, and his correspondence with his solicitor, Mr Miles Walker, which ended in her claim to the relationship being found perfectly valid. We also have a copy of Mr Railsdon's letter to Miss Raymond in which he suggested a meeting in London.'

'Well, the first time I heard of her existence was when he got back from London after this meeting. He came over here and told me the whole story.'

'Considering that you are getting married in the near future, weren't you surprised that he hadn't told you before?'

'Just for a few minutes I felt a bit hurt. Naturally I want to share his worries and difficulties. But he explained that he had hoped to be able to keep the whole business quiet by making Laura an allowance, and letting her feel that she could get any further help from him that she needed. He assured me that he was going to tell me about her when things were fixed up. But as you know, she wanted both more and less than that, if I'm making myself clear.'

'Perfectly clear, Miss Legge,' Pollard replied. 'Why do you think Mr Railsdon was so anxious to hush up her existence?'

'He thought the situation was – well, discreditable to

his father. He was very fond of his father. Then he felt it could be unpleasant for both of us, and also for his daughter, and that the constituency Conservative party might regret having nominated him as their candidate for the next election.'

'How did you react to these anxieties of his?'

'My first reaction was that he was making rather heavy weather of it all. I mean, the majority of people seem to take illegitimacy in their stride these days, don't they? But when he told me more about Laura I could see that meeting her wish to be considered one of the family was going to make a lot of difficulties. But I felt very sorry for her, and also that the Railsdons – and I'm about to become one myself – had, well, a moral responsibility towards her. He also said that she wasn't a fool by any means, and would quite possibly see for herself that she was a hopeless misfit socially and settle for the allowance suggestion. This seemed to me to make sense, and anyway I said I felt it had been a good idea to get her down here, and that of course I'd do everything I could to help.'

'And when she arrived?' Pollard asked.

'It was much more difficult than I expected,' Henrietta replied frankly.

'There was a small family supper party on the Tuesday evening, wasn't there?'

'Yes. I was there, and so was Jeremy Crabbe, Amanda Railsdon's fiancé. It was appallingly heavy going. We all did our level best to draw Laura in, so to speak, but it really was no go. It wasn't so much because of her accent and her table manners and whatever, but on account of her limitations. She didn't seem able to join in any general conversation whatever, and every topic dried up after about half-a-minute. The only subject that got a spark out of her was cars.

164

Apparently she had a Mini, and had admired the Hyperion on the way back from Shirborough station. Basil had said he'd take her for a drive the next morning, and suggested that she should bring the car round herself, at half past ten. He'd meant to start at ten, but Tom Whitworth rang up in the middle of supper wanting to see Basil urgently, so it had to be ten-thirty.'

'What happened after supper?'

'We had coffee in the drawing-room, and then Basil took Laura round to the feedstore to show her how to start up the Hyperion. I didn't think that I should be helping matters by staying around, so I said I had things to do at home and came back here in my own car. I never saw Laura again until . . .'

'Until you found her body in the feedstore at about half past ten the next morning?'

Henrietta nodded assent. They sat without speaking for a few moments.

'An appalling experience for you, I'm afraid,' Pollard commented. 'The Shirborough police were impressed by the presence of mind you showed, Miss Legge. I'm sorry to have had to dig it all up again, but this talk we've had has been helpful.'

'I'm afraid I must sound an absolutely ghastly snob,' Henrietta said. 'I really was sorry for her. The way she spoke and ate and all that wasn't her fault. It wouldn't have mattered anything like as much if she'd been different in herself.'

'What was it in her that you found so difficult to take?'

'She was terribly bitter and resented us. Perhaps that was understandable. What I couldn't take was that I felt she knew perfectly well how she was jarring on us and was enjoying it in a malicious sort of way. I thought it was as if it gave her a sense of power.'

*　　　*　　　*

165

'Do you think Miss Legge had cottoned on to the idea that Raymond had blackmailed Railsdon into having her down?' Toye asked as they walked back to the Rover.

'I wondered, of course, Pollard replied. 'I even debated asking her flat out but came down against it. On the whole I doubt it. She's obviously intelligent and perceptive, but in the rather closed county society she's lived in, blackmail's something non-U that happens in the world outside. And if the idea had ever flitted across her mind there'd have been a potent subconscious drive to stifle it at birth. Didn't you notice the signs of hard-upness in that room? Worn upholstery and faded curtains, for instance. Railsdon's offering her security backed up by plenty of cash . . . Look here, thanks to the Tremlett-Browns we're now in a position to work out a reasonably accurate timetable of people's movements last Wednesday morning. I'd like to do it before tackling Railsdon. Let's find a pull-in a bit beyond the Loxford House gates.'

Five minutes later they had parked in a lay-by on the Mallingham Road.

'The crucial time,' Pollard said, writing rapidly in his notebook, 'is from just before a quarter to ten when the T-Bs are prepared to swear that the feedstore door was open and no one was crossing the meadow, to just about ten-ten, when they swear it was shut and once again nobody was visible in the meadow. Let's start with Miss Legge.'

Toye's notes confirmed that the Tremlett-Browns had both seen Miss Legge and heard her hoovering an upstairs room in Abbey Cottage on their arrival at just after nine-twenty-five. They had spent a little time inspecting the outside of the cottage they had come to view before unlocking it and going in, at – say –

166

nine-thirty-three. Would she have had time to get up to the feedstore, shut and fasten the door on Laura Raymond, and get back to her garden by just after nine-forty-five without the T-Bs seeing her returning across the meadow?

'It simply isn't on,' Pollard said. Toye, habitually cautious, concurred.

'All right. Now then, to recap. The T-Bs saw her about in the garden of Abbey Cottage up to just before ten when they went to the end of the cul-de-sac, looked at the meadow, and saw that somebody had shut the feedstore door. We agree that it couldn't have been Miss Legge. But from ten-ten onwards she was unobserved. She says she noticed that the door was shut when washing her hands at about ten-twenty before setting out across the meadow, but that she didn't notice anyone about in it. Now we come to the odd business of her finding the door shut, but not secured by the staple and hasp, when she reached the feedstore en route for Loxford House. How come?'

'Either it never was fastened, and Raymond died because she thought it was and became hysterical. Or A.N. Other who had shut and fastened it in the first place, returned to unhook the staple between ten-ten and ten-twenty approx., to give the impression that the door never had been fastened. Or Miss Legge was lying just now to protect A.N. Other and unfastened the door herself to make it look like an accident, so to speak.'

They sat in silence for nearly a minute.

'Let's face it,' Pollard said abruptly. 'We aren't getting anywhere really significant in this bloody case, are we? All we've done so far is to eliminate Amanda Railsdon, Cobbledick, kids and local nutcases, and prove that Henrietta Legge couldn't have shut Raymond into the feedstore. There's no proof that she found the door unfastened when she passed on her way to Loxford House at about half past ten: we've only her word for it. We've no proof whatever that Mrs Bennett is speaking the truth about what she was doing after taking Railsdon's breakfast into the dining-room at about nine-fifteen. We haven't tackled Railsdon himself yet. I think we shall be able to prove he had ample opportunity to pull off the job, but don't forget that so far we haven't established a motive that would stand up in court – in the unlikely event of the case getting past the D.P.P. Perhaps we ought to have started off by making enquiries in Medstone about Raymond's temperament and general mental state. But damn it all, Shirborough asked the Yard to take over the enquiry because they jibbed at the possibility of getting embroiled with Railsdon and the True Blues of the constituency, and the A.C. picked on us and told us to come down here, didn't he?'

Toye conceded the point, adding that he didn't see what else they could have done.

'All right,' Pollard resumed. 'We'll go to Loxford House, tackle Railsdon, possibly have a word with his daughter and then hit the trail for Town. Put in an interim report, have an evening and night at home, and go down to Medstone tomorrow morning. If we draw a blank there I'll report again to the A.C. and suggest that there's insufficient proof for anything but an open verdict at the resumed inquest.'

Toye glanced at him, decided against any attempt at optimism, and reluctantly reversed the Rover. Two minutes later they turned into the drive of Loxford House. He slowed down.

'One thing that seems odd to me,' he said tentatively, 'is why Raymond went over to the feedstore so early, assuming that she opened it up in the first place. She wasn't due to take the car round till half past ten because of Whitworth's date with Railsdon.'

'It's a point,' Pollard agreed, 'but one's got to try to think oneself into her skin. Nobody wants to look a fool, and in her place I'd have wanted to make sure I remembered what Railsdon had told me about starting up the Hyperion or whatever. I think she may very well have slipped down that staircase leading to the kitchen and out into the yard while Bennett was taking in Railsdon's breakfast, and then gone for a stroll once she felt she could cope with the car. This could explain why Railsdon still hadn't shut her in by a quarter to ten – if he ever did. He'd have been lurking behind the building waiting for her to come back, and keeping an eye on his watch because of Whitworth. It still doesn't explain how he could have banked on her not switching off the engine. Hell! Let's scrub it *pro tem*. That looks like young Amanda outside the house.'

Amanda Railsdon in white jeans and an exiguous scarlet top was playing with a young golden labrador which she grabbed by the collar as Toye drew up. She gave them an enquiring look as Pollard got out and introduced himself and Toye.

'I thought it must be you,' she said. 'Your car's a talking point in the village. The mechanically-minded say it has a souped-up engine . . . I expect you want my father, don't you?'

She was most attractive, Pollard thought, and positively glowing with vitality and happiness. Crabbe was a lucky young blighter . . .

'We should be glad of a word with him,' he replied. 'Is he at home?'

'He's gone into Mallingham to the bank, but ought to be back any time now. I can't think what's held him up.

Would you like to sit in the garden and wait for a bit?'
She indicated a group of garden chairs, and put the
puppy on a lead, explaining that they had only had him
for two days. 'Our darling old one had to be put to
sleep in May at the age of seventeen, and we couldn't
face starting with a new one right away.'

They settled in the luxuriously comfortable chairs
and talked easily about dogs and the Pollards' little
black cat Nox. Suddenly Amanda broke off and gave
Pollard a long steady look.

'This ghastly business about Laura Raymond's too
utterly grim,' she said. 'I somehow feel it's bound to
rub off on us for keeps. On Daddy and Henrietta anyway, as they'll be living here. I shan't be around so
much when Jeremy and I are married.'

'What happened, in your opinion?' Pollard asked
her.

'Of course I know the police have to delve into
things, but it seems obvious to me – to all of us. The
door must have swung shut because Laura hadn't propped it open properly, and she thought she couldn't
open it again and became hysterical instead of switching off the engine. It does need a bit of a push sometimes because gravel gets underneath. It sounds absolutely bonkers, of course, but she was a pretty odd sort
of person, you know.'

'Odd in what sort of way?'

Amanda was silent for a few moments, contemplating the toes of her left foot which protruded from a
scarlet sandal.

'Don't get me wrong,' she said earnestly. 'I was
frightfully sorry for her and wanted to help her to – to
unwind. Of course you know what a rotten deal she and
her mother had from my grandfather. I think he was
the utter end, casting her off like that. But to be abso-

170

lutely honest I began to feel after just one afternoon that she'd been damaged beyond repair. Psychologically, I mean. It stuck out a mile that she resented and loathed us, and yet she was simply hell-bent on coming to live on the doorstep just to make things difficult for us.'

'Did she actually say that she wanted to come and live on the doorstep?' Out of the corner of his eye Pollard saw Toye unobtrusively taking notes.

'Not actually in those words, but she made it quite plain. It was when I was taking her round the garden after tea on the day she came down here. You can see Henrietta Legge's cottage if you're standing near the feedstore, and she asked who it belonged to. When I told her, and explained that Daddy and Henrietta are giving it to Jeremy and me as a wedding present, she started to ask a lot of nosey questions. What his job was, and if we were really going to live there and so on. And then she asked if Daddy owned any other cottages in the village. It stood out a mile what she was thinking . . . Oh, here is Daddy at last! What can he have been doing all this time?'

The Hyperion drew up alongside the Rover, and a tall, fair man got out and came towards the group on the lawn. Pollard's first impressions were of good looks and assurance, but as Basil Railsdon approached it was clear that he looked shaken.

'Daddy, what's happened?' Amanda demanded before Pollard could introduce himself.

'It's O.K., darling. Just rather a narrow squeak on the road, that's all . . . Chief Superintendent Pollard, isn't it, and . . .?'

'My colleague, Inspector Toye. I'm so sorry you've . . .'

'Daddy, what actually happened?' Amanda cut in.

171

'A sudden puncture,' her father replied. 'On the straight, after you come through Littleford. I was going a bit of a lick and the tyre suddenly went. It was damn all I could do to keep her on the road and clear of the oncoming traffic, and I ended up inches behind a whacking great van ahead of me,' he concluded, subsiding into a chair.

A strangled sound came from Toye.

'A puncture on that car!' he exclaimed. 'Why, Sir, it's an X registration. How long have you had it?'

Basil Railsdon looked at him and grinned.

'Just three months, Inspector. It really is a bit rum. The van driver turned out trumps, and insisted on helping me change the wheel. We had a look at it, and one of the grooves in the nearside front tyre looks as though it's been enlarged, and there's a hole underneath. Small, but quite deep. The bloke's comment was "vandals", prefixed by a string of adjectives which I'll omit. But it seems a bit subtle for vandalism, don't you think? Broken windows and damaged coachwork are the usual thing.'

'Inspector Toye's holding on to the seat of his chair,' Pollard remarked. 'Cars are his top thing. Could he have a look?'

'Why, of course. I'd be interested to have his opinion. It's in the spare wheel space at the bottom of the boot, Inspector, which I regret to admit isn't locked . . . I know it's not on to offer you both a drink, Chief Superintendent, but I feel acutely in need of one myself. Mandy darling, could you bear to get me a spot of whisky?'

'Prompt service is our speciality', she replied, and ran off, the young labrador capering at her side.

Toye, who had hurried off, was in the process of extracting the tyre from the Hyperion. They watched

172

him fetch a small case from the Rover and sit down on the front steps.

'He's using a lens,' Pollard said. 'We always have a fairly powerful one handy.'

As Toye became increasingly absorbed Amanda reappeared with a glass on a small tray.

'I'll fade out now,' she announced, 'and take Rollo up the woods to work off some of his surplus energy. Goodbye, Chief Superintendent. It's been a thrill to meet you, and I can tell Jeremy it's honours even now. He's been bragging about being interviewed by a Yard Ace.'

'Spare me, Miss Railsdon,' Pollard said, 'and thank you for your help.'

As she ran off Toye rejoined them.

'You've been lucky, Sir,' he told Basil Railsdon. 'There's quite a bit of the outer covering missing. You must have driven over something sharp like a flint, maybe, and by bad luck it got into the slit and went right through to the canvas and the inner tube. Very nasty it could have been if you hadn't managed to keep control the way you did. I'd rather like Shirborough to take a look. They've got the equipment to make a really thorough examination. What do you say, Sir?' he asked Pollard with official formality.

Years of close cooperation between them enabled Pollard to come in on this cue.

'I'm inclined to agree,' he said. 'It looks a bit off-beat. What do you feel, Mr Railsdon? It's your property. We can drop the tyre in at Shirborough police station for you, if you like?'

'One bloody thing after another,' Basil commented, putting down an empty glass. 'Sorry, Inspector. That sounds ungracious. I'm grateful for your help, and I agree the damage ought to be investigated in the public interest, not to mention my own over an insurance claim . . . I take it this is an official visit, Chief Superintendent? Shall we go into the house? I'm feeling more *compos mentis* after that drink.'

As they walked across the hall Pollard's eye picked out a magnificent chest of carved oak, and Persian rugs on the floor which he felt it almost sacrilegious to walk over. The study was functional but also contrived to suggest affluence. After they had sat down Basil Railsdon looked at him enquiringly.

'As you haven't cautioned me, I presume that you haven't come along to charge me with my half-sister's murder? I admit that I haven't an alibi, of course.'

'Actually you have the makings of one,' Pollard replied. 'Quite a lot has happened this morning. We've come along to see if you can fill in some gaps. We called on Miss Legge at her home and found a rather tiresome couple there who were trying to pressurise her into selling them her cottage. It turned out that on the morning of Miss Raymond's death they were viewing the empty cottage just opposite. I needn't trouble you with a lot of unnecessary detail, but both are prepared to state on oath that they saw the door of the feedstore open and a vehicle inside at a quarter to ten, and that when they looked at it again at ten o'clock or just after, it had been shut. As Miss Legge was seen by them in her garden during the whole of this period she could not have shut it. Please,' – Pollard held up his hand authoritatively to check the expected outburst – 'a man with your experience of the world must surely know what is involved in a police enquiry, although I understand your reaction at this moment.'

He watched the anger in Basil Railsdon's face give place to relief. But all the same, was there an underlying anxiety?

174

'Of course, I know you've got a job to do, Chief Superintendent. But apart from the outrageous idea of Miss Legge being involved in a murder, what I find so infuriating about all this is that there would be absolutely no point in anyone shutting Miss Raymond into the feedstore unless they knew for certain that she wouldn't immediately switch off the Hyperion's engine. Obviously her death was an accident, either because the door stuck in some way or because she had some sort of brainstorm and didn't try to get out.'

'All this has been considered and gone into carefully, Mr Railsdon,' Pollard replied mildly. 'The whereabouts of every child in the village on that Wednesday morning has been checked in case the tragedy was a joke that misfired. The vicar tells me that there are no mentally disturbed people in the village. Inspector Toye and I will be in Medstone tomorrow discussing Miss Raymond's health with her doctor, and getting the opinion of her employer and others on her mental state. Before we leave we have come to see if you can produce any confirmation of your statement that you spent the whole of the period between nine-thirty and ten o'clock in this study. I suppose no one put through a telephone call to you?'

'I wish to God they had. No, nobody rang me.'

'Did you ring anyone yourself?'

'I had two goes, but couldn't get an answer.'

'Did you ring the same number each time?'

'Yes. I was trying to contact my part-time typist.'

'May we have her name, address and telephone number? Quite possibly somebody heard the phone ringing.'

Basil stared at him.

'God, I never thought of that.' He scribbled on a sheet of writing-paper. 'I rang quite early on, as soon as

175

I'd looked through my mail and seen that there were a number of letters that had to be answered. Say twenty to ten. Then I thought it was worth having another bash not long before Whitworth was due: between ten and five minutes to ten, I should think.'

'Thank you, Mr Railsdon,' Pollard took the piece of paper held out to him and passed it to Toye. 'We shall get Inspector Blair to cope with this. His chaps will have the advantage of local knowledge. And now Inspector Toye and I must be getting along.'

'Sorry if I've been a bit abrasive,' Basil said as he escorted them to the front door, 'but honestly all this has been a bit much to take, especially as one feels that a lot of the ground that's been covered is plain irrelevant in view of the running car engine factor. Still, I see you're bound to go into every alternative to start off with . . . By the way, the cremation's on Friday, and Laura's ashes are being buried in the churchyard here at three. She'd expressed a wish to be cremated in her Will. Her solicitor's her executor and he's coming down, so if you want to see him he won't be in Medstone that day. Webster's the name, but you'll have had all the gen from Inspector Blair, of course.'

Pollard glanced in the driving mirror as the Rover moved off. Basil Railsdon stood on the steps watching their departure, a rather oddly rigid figure, he thought, and turned to Toye.

'What was behind your smooth patter about that tyre? Do you seriously think that it was malicious damage with the aim of liquidating Railsdon?'

Toye, as always, was cautious.

'I reckon it's possible,' he replied. 'The lens showed up quite clearly that a sharp knife of some sort had been used to enlarge the groove, and something a bit bigger to dig out the hole underneath. One can't be

176

more definite without better lighting and a blown-up photograph.'

'We'll push it over to Blair, then . . . My God, you see the possible implication of course? It could mean that Railsdon was the intended victim, not Laura Raymond, I suppose, although we're still confronted with the problem of the Hyperion's engine being left running.'

'A chap in Railsdon's position must have made enemies along the way,' Toye propounded. 'Business rivals, and even political enemies, come to that.'

'I can't quite see political hostility going to those lengths in a constituency like North Crantshire,' Pollard said thoughtfully. 'We'll get the Yard to make a few enquiries about Railsdon, though.'

After a rather silent drive to Shirborough they parked at police headquarters and went in search of Inspector Blair, who was obviously gratified when asked if he would spare them a little time. Pollard proceeded to bring him up to date.

'Of course this business of the damaged tyre may have absolutely nothing to do with Laura Raymond's death,' he concluded, 'but we're pretty well stymied over that at the moment, so we'd be glad if your technicians could have a go. And if by a stroke of sheer luck somebody happened to hear Miss Hookway's telephone ringing twice between nine-thirty and ten last Wednesday at the times Railsdon claims to have rung her, he'd be a write-off as far as I can see.'

Blair promised to put his chaps on to both jobs without delay.

'Roselea Court where this Miss Hookway lives is a newish block of flats,' he said. 'Probably the sound insulation is rotten, and there's a chance of fed-up neighbours having noticed her phone going. About the funeral, Sir. Would you like me to attend if you and Inspector Toye aren't back?'

'Unless something quite unforeseen crops up we'll drive down on Friday morning. Assume we're coming if I don't ring you from the Yard at about nine on Friday morning. And perhaps you'd let us know if you have any luck over the telephone enquiry. The Yard will take a message if I'm out. Here's the number, and ask for Extension 17.'

Blair went off to detail his underlings, highly pleased at the prospect of putting through a call to Scotland Yard. Pollard and Toye rang their respective homes to announce their return at some stage during the evening, and after a hasty snack took the London road. The inevitable pile-up of desk-work awaited them, and it was after seven when Pollard inserted his latch-key into the Yale lock of his front door in Wimbledon. Simultaneously his wife Jane appeared from the kitchen.

'Jordan passed, anyway temporarily,' he said, releasing her from a bear's hug. 'Everything O.K.?'

'Everything. I promised the twins you'd ring them if you got in before nine. What would you like to do first? Supper's ready in the slow oven.'

'I'll have a shower and get into a clean shirt, first, I think, and then ring the kids. Then at long last we can relax.'

'Good. You've got that odd operational smell: some sort of disinfectant they spray with at the Yard, perhaps.'

'Don't ever mention it to Toye, for God's sake. He'll think you're casting aspersions on the Rover,' Pollard replied from the stairs.

Andrew and Rose Pollard, the ten-and-a-half-year-old twins, were staying with Pollard's brother on his Sussex farm, and gave an ecstatic account of their activities. Everything, apparently, was super. Pollard finally managed to bring the call to an end, and returned to the kitchen to find Jane putting a shoulder of lamb encircled with roast potatoes on the table.

'This is it,' he commented, sinking on to his chair and taking up the carvers. 'I've had nothing but a cuppa since a lousy snack in the Shirborough canteen before we started back about one o'clock.'

'How long are you home for?' Jane asked. 'Don't give me the whole joint, darling. And only two potatoes. Middle-aged spread is looming if I'm not careful.'

'O.K. Now I'm going to help myself *ad lib* . . . Until early Friday morning, with luck.'

'I'd hoped from what you guardedly said over the line that it looked like being a non-case and there was a chance of it fizzling out.'

'So there was, but there's been a rather odd development and now I'm not so sure. I suppose you've been following the case in the papers?'

'Of course. I always do. It's compulsive reading as far as I'm concerned. The twins are getting hooked, too.'

'Good Lord!' Pollard paused, a laden fork half-way to his mouth. 'For heaven's sake try to head them off the more appalling ones.'

'No way,' Jane replied. 'They'd smell a rat and get hold of the papers somehow. Don't worry, though. At present it's just cops and robbers to them, and with clever Daddy as Super Cop. And incidentally, I've got a super bit of news for you.'

He looked enquiring, and took the letter she passed to him.

'Aunt Is!' he said in surprise, recognising the businesslike heading and impeccable typing of his favourite aunt's correspondence.

179

'Read on,' Jane urged.

The letter was short and to the point. Nearly eleven years ago, on hearing that Jane was about to produce twins, Miss Isabel Dennis M.B.E. had promptly taken out an educational insurance policy. As from the twins' eleventh birthday the sum of £500 would be paid to their parents on the first of January and the first of July each year, over a period of five years.

'*This should help,*' Miss Dennis had written. '*I commend your good sense in choosing a place to live in with such excellent day schools . . .*'

'Not only a tax-free thousand a year towards the fees,' Pollard commented, 'but a pat on the back thrown in. A positive accolade.'

'I hope to heaven she'll feel it's been money well spent at the end of the day,' Jane said. 'Anyway I needn't take on any more work at the College of Art and they needn't be latch-key kids, thank goodness, unless the fees go progressively through the roof.'

'Of course Rose may get a scholarship on her art . . .'

The evening passed happily in an optimistic review of the family's finance and plans, and the composition of a joint letter to Miss Isabel Dennis, Loxford and its problems receding for the time being to the back of Pollard's mind. They were brought back abruptly, however, by a telephone call just before ten o'clock.

'A message from Shirborough police headquarters, Sir,' a voice from the Yard informed him. 'Detective-Inspector Blair reports that he has obtained confirmation of two unanswered telephone calls to Miss Pamela Hookway's flat in Roselea Court, Shirborough, on the morning of Wednesday of last week at about 0940 and 0955 hours respectively. End of message.'

'Thanks,' Pollard said. 'I've got that.'

'It *is* a case,' he told Jane, 'and refuses to go away as unsolvable. We'll have to go down on Friday morning, though what exactly for I haven't a clue at the moment.'

Chapter Eight

Medstone, which was new ground to Pollard, proved to be a sprawling outer suburb with no recognisable town plan. Toye had acquired a street map, and they began operations by a visit to the police station in the main street. This proved almost entirely abortive. After getting a telephone call from Inspector Blair reporting Miss Raymond's death, Inspector Worth of Medstone had sent a constable round to the house. The key had been borrowed from a Mrs Rank next door, and she had gone over the house with the constable. Everything was in perfect order, and nothing relating to the visit to Loxford House had been found. Mrs Rank had said that Miss Raymond and her mother had kept very much to themselves and had no close friends. After Mr Webster, the solicitor, had rung up, saying he was Miss Raymond's executor, the constable had acted as escort again, but it seemed that Mr Webster had been mainly concerned with what the house and its contents would fetch.

Realising that nothing further was to be gained by prolonging the interview Pollard asked if he could telephone the office of Webster and Treat, Laura Raymond's solicitors. He made an appointment to see Mr

Webster in an hour's time, and left the police station for Seabright's, the large department store where she had been employed. It appeared prosperous and busy, and he presented his card at a desk carrying the notice ENQUIRIES, having added 'Re the late Miss Raymond'. The young woman who accepted it goggled at him and hastily rang a bell. An older woman appeared, took one glance at the card and requested Pollard to follow.

The Manager's office was on the first floor, and after a brief delay Pollard and Toye were ushered in. An energetic-looking man of about fifty rose from behind a huge desk covered with files and papers and introduced himself as John Marsh.

'My colleague, Detective-Inspector Toye,' Pollard said, indicating his companion as they sat down facing the desk.

'I thought someone would come along sooner or later,' John Marsh commented after refreshments and cigarettes had been offered and politely refused. 'Quite extraordinary the interest poor old Raymond's exit's arousing in the press. But there's precious little help I can give you, I'm afraid, beyond what you obviously know already about her having worked here for nearly twenty years.'

'You may be able to help us more than you think, Mr Marsh,' Pollard told him. 'What we are trying to find out is what sort of a person she was.'

'Well,' John Marsh replied, 'a potted biography of her as an employee of this joint is probably the best I can do for you. She was here when I came ten years ago, and had worked her way up to being senior assistant in the Household Equipment Department. The store had just been taken over by House of Henderson, and they'd put me in to carry out a planned expansion

183

and galvanise the show generally. So I spent quite a bit of time hanging around watching people on their jobs and customer reaction. I was struck by Raymond's competence over stock and display and whatever, but she was obviously a bit short on human contacts. So when I'd got the hang of things we had a major re-organisation, and I decided to put her in as general stock manager in place of an old buffer who was due to be pensioned off.'

'How long ago was this?' Pollard asked.

'Eight years this autumn; and it's been completely justified. I've found her entirely reliable. I picked her the right sort of assistants: people who knew how to work and had a head for figures like her, and the whole store's benefited. There was feeling, of course, in some quarters. The transfer nearly doubled her salary, for one thing. A few of 'em who were senior to her when she was promoted came along to protest in a bunch, but I told them there was nobody on the door to stop 'em walking out if they felt like it, and the rumpus soon died down.'

'I suppose,' Pollard pursued, 'that in a big store like this you have staff clubs and various social events?'

'That's right, and Raymond never showed up except at the Annual Dinner. I put my foot down over that. Everybody's expected to be there, from myself downwards.'

'Did her refusal to join in the various activities make her unpopular?'

'No,' John Marsh replied after brief consideration. 'I wouldn't say that. She was just written off as a bit of a freak. Her clothes and the fact that she left her face and hair as Nature made 'em were seen as bearing this out. It was generally known that she had an elderly and delicate mother to look after, which was taken as a sort of explanation. Raymond bought a small, second-hand car after her big rise in salary and I've met her on the road at weekends with an elderly lady once or twice.'

'You've been very helpful, Mr Marsh,' Pollard said, 'and I'm going to take you into our confidence, which I feel sure you'll respect. Miss Raymond's death has raised a number of questions. The circumstances surrounding it are puzzling. One suggestion is that the door of the building, which was being used as a temporary garage, closed of its own accord or from being blown to by the wind, and if she hadn't panicked she could have got out perfectly well. Did she ever, to your knowledge, show any signs of being hysterical? Was she the type you'd expect to lose her head and go to pieces in a sudden emergency?'

John Marsh leant back in his chair and surveyed his questioner.

'You can scrub any idea of that sort, Chief Superintendent, right now. Raymond was as cool as a cucumber in an unexpected crisis. There was a small fire in one of the stock-rooms a few years ago, due to an electrical fault. In no time at all she'd sounded the store alarm system, had every window shut and the whole floor evacuated, and was operating an extinguisher when the store fire team arrived. Then there was another occasion when we had an I.R.A. bomb scare. Her lot were the first to come down the fire escape and line up in the yard. She had her faults like the rest of us, but she had guts right enough and knew how to keep her head. And she was physically strong – remarkably so for her height. It's impossible to imagine her not being able to shove open a garage door that had closed on her. Unless somebody had fastened it from outside, of course. I've seen her heaving whacking great packages about.'

185

From the bustle of Seabright's superstore and the traffic jams of Medstone's main shopping street, Pollard and Toye located Mr Webster's office in a relatively quiet side road in which some large Edwardian houses had survived. The firm of Webster and Treat occupied the ground floor of one of these. Mr Webster, as Miles Walker had told Basil Railsdon, clearly did not operate in the higher echelons of the legal profession, but he gave an impression of being perfectly competent in the day-to-day matters handled by a solicitor. A tin box labelled RAYMOND had been placed on his desk in preparation for the interview. As Pollard had feared, however, he had very little information to offer about his late client, with whom he had had minimal personal contact.

'The firm handled the purchase of the house in Alexandra Road when Mrs Raymond moved down here in 1947. That was just a few months before I came in. After that we've no record of any further transactions on either her or her daughter's behalf until Miss Raymond contacted me just before last Christmas, saying that her mother had died and that her Will was with us. We offered her an appointment, and found the Will with the deeds of the house in this box, and saw that Mrs Raymond had made the firm her executors. That was the first time I saw Miss Raymond. She came along and was perfectly sensible about the necessary procedures, and asked us to act for her. We agreed, of course, and went ahead. It was a very simple Will, her mother having left her everything she possessed unconditionally. We got probate in due course and wound up the estate. Miss Raymond then asked us to draw up her own Will. This also was a very short, simple one. She expressed a wish to be cremated, and left everything she died possessed of to Dr Barnado's, without any strings attached, and, as her mother had done, she appointed this firm her executors. We let her know when it was ready, she came along to sign it, and eventually we sent her an account which she paid at once. I never saw her again, or heard anything about her until a Mr Miles Walker, Mr Basil Railsdon's solicitor, contacted me, and told me about her death, and also about her relationship to Mr Railsdon. As we are the executors I went over the house, and brought away the few business papers I found – bank statements and receipts and so on. I'm afraid that's all I've got to tell you, Chief Superintendent,' Mr Webster concluded.

'What did you make of Miss Raymond as a person?' Pollard asked.

'She wasn't what is generally called an educated person,' Mr Webster said thoughtfully, 'but she struck me as being very competent over business affairs, and when she told me of the post she held at Seabright's it confirmed this impression. She must undoubtedly have been earning a very good salary, and over and above that her mother had left her a useful little bit of capital.. Because money obviously wasn't a problem I wondered why she had neglected her personal appearance so badly. I thought her brusqueness covered some basic unhappiness, and after I had heard her history from Mr Walker it was easy to see what this could have been.'

'Did she strike you as neurotic? Likely to go to pieces under stress?'

'Far from it. She seemed to me a stolid and determined woman.'

'There's one other matter we're interested in, Mr Webster,' Pollard told him. 'Did she say anything to you about her future plans?'

'Not directly,' the solicitor replied. 'She said that she had seen in the local paper that houses identical to her own in Alexandra Road were selling for between twenty and thirty thousand pounds. Did I think this could be true? Her mother had paid five hundred pounds for hers in 1947. I said that I should expect that to be the price range, but of course a good deal would depend on the condition of the house and how far it had been modernised.'

'She didn't say that she was proposing to sell?'

'No, and I didn't ask her outright, but I said that we should be glad to give her any help she needed if she decided on a sale at any time.'

'You are going down to her funeral tomorrow, I think?' Pollard asked.

'Yes,' Mr Webster replied. 'As representing her executors. Mr Railsdon has kindly offered to meet my train at Shirborough and give me lunch. Perhaps we shall meet again, then?'

'We shall be at the church for the interment of the ashes,' Pollard told him. 'Like yourself, in an official capacity. As you've no doubt gathered, the enquiry into Miss Raymond's death is anything but complete.'

They left shortly afterwards for the final stage of their enquiries in Medstone. Alexandra Road appeared, from the street plan, to be part of a housing development on the west side of the town, and they collected the Rover from the car park at the police station and drove out to it. The houses had been laid out in small terraces, and had minute front gardens and rather larger ones at the back. The Raymonds', Number 30, looked in good condition. Heads appeared at nearby windows as Pollard and Toye got out and let themselves into the house with the key lent by Mr Webster. It had been left in impeccable order, and it looked as though Laura Raymond had spent some of her increased income on modern equipment such as a Rayburn and

188

night storage heaters. Paintwork and wallpapers were fresh, even if the latter were, to Pollard's mind, frankly hideous. There were two comfortable chairs in the little front sitting-room, and a television set. But in spite of these amenities he found the atmosphere sterile rather than cosy. There was little sign of anyone having enjoyed living there: a mere dozen books on a shelf and a few stereotyped prints on the walls. The back garden had been paved. Some plants in pots were dotted about and were drooping from lack of water.

Mr Webster had investigated an imitation oak bureau, and Pollard and Toye agreed that nothing of the slightest relevance to Laura Raymond's visit to Loxford had been overlooked. They found a modest quantity of uninspired clothing in her bedroom, but no letters or diary concealed in any of the orderly piles of serviceable garments in the chest of drawers. They searched the wardrobe and its contents, and finally pulled off the bed-cover and examined the folded blankets and the mattress. Pollard threw down a pillow in a sudden spasm of irritability.

'What the hell are we expecting to find, anyway? A pocket diary with "*Decided to blackmail Basil Railsdon*" as the entry for April the first?'

He took a couple of steps across to the window and stood looking down at the lifeless little garden and the backs of the houses in the next road. It's like a prison cell, he thought, where a lifetime's resentment and frustration has festered in isolation. Behind him Toye, engaged in neatly refolding blankets, uncharacteristically remarked that the place somehow gave him the willies.

They left shortly afterwards, still under stealthy observation from behind curtains, and after returning the key to Mr Webster's office set off for the Yard.

189

'Well,' Pollard said, once they were on the road, 'what have we got out of this trip, if anything?'

'There's no proof one way or the other,' Toye replied as he drew up at a red traffic light, 'but it looks as though it's a case of homicide all right. If that chap Marsh spoke the truth about Raymond keeping her cool in a crisis, I can't see her panicking over a door that you had to shove a bit to open. I reckon somebody'd slipped the staple into the hasp.'

'I'm with you that far,' Pollard said as they began to move slowly forward, 'but if she was all that cool and collected why on earth didn't she switch off the Hyperion's engine? Damn it all, she was a car-owner herself. And another little problem needing our attention is, who fastened the door? Not Legge, and as far as I can see, not Railsdon. I suppose we'd better get down to grilling Bennett.'

Toye admitted that things looked a bit baffling at the moment, but the forensic blokes down at Shirborough might have got on to something over the tyre business.

Back at the Yard Pollard added a précis of the interviews at Medstone to his reports for the A.C., who, he was relieved to hear, was attending a top level conference due to last over the following day.

'We'll take off early for Shirborough,' he told Toye. 'I'm certain in my own mind that Raymond was bumped off, and why the hell should whoever did it get away with an open verdict?'

*　　　*　　　*

'Our chaps have gone to town on that tyre of Railsdon's,' Inspector Blair told Pollard and Toye when they arrived at Shirborough the following morning. 'But what it's going to add up to's anybody's guess, I'd say. Come along to the lab.'

The Shirborough forensic laboratory was small but well-equipped. The two technicians had been put on their mettle

190

by the unexpected chance of doing a job for a Chief Superintendent from the Yard, and their findings were laid out in readiness. They were introduced as Sergeant Thirsk and Constable May.

Pollard and Toye pored over a series of enormously blown-up photographs.

'To our minds there's no doubt at all that the damage was deliberate, Sir,' Sergeant Thirsk told Pollard. 'Just take a look at this one. You can see how the groove in the rubber's been lengthened by about a centimetre if you compare it with the ones next to it. A sliver's been shaved off on each side by a sharp knife, but not quite evenly, see? Then the bottom of the enlarged groove was cut through . . . The next photograph shows the digging down with some small sharp tool.'

'Yes, it's perfectly clear,' Pollard said. 'And the hole broadens out a bit as it goes down.'

'The sides get rougher, too,' Toye pointed out. 'Whoever dug it out must have wedged the slit open. Take the wedge away, and the slit would close up again, hiding the hole.'

The succeeding phtographs showed what looked like a narrow, ragged shaft running vertically downwards to the canvas and splitting the surface of the inner-tube.'

'That's what caused the blow-out, Sir,' Sergeant Thirsk said, 'and here's what actually did the job.'

Constable May produced a large rusty nail and brought forward the dismantled tyre for examination.

'Then if you'd step this way, Sir, we'll show you what we managed to get out of the hole.'

A microscope and some slides awaited them on the next bench. The first of these, Pollard and Toye were told, showed a deposit taken from the undamaged outer surface of the tyre, and consisted of mud with minute fragments of grit and vegetable matter. A sample taken from the sides of the original groove had been analysed and found to contain asphalt. Finally, from the hole itself, some tiny pieces of eggshell thinness had been extracted and identified as part of a plastic substance. This, the technicians thought, had been curved. The fragments were blue on one side and white on the other.

Pollard and Toye were warm in their congratulations to the technicians, and Inspector Blair concealed his pride in their achievement by casually remarking that he was glad that the boys had managed to come up with something.

'It's not ordinary vandalism,' Pollard said, reverting to the display of photographs. 'Much too skilled and subtle for the average basher and smasher. Possibly an attempt to involve whoever drove the car in an accident, but I'm doubtful.'

There was general agreement that it would be a pretty unreliable method of liquidating anybody.

'You couldn't be sure of a puncture for some time,' Blair argued, 'and even then it might happen when the car was moving quite slowly and easy to control. And even if someone had it in for Railsdon there could have been passengers on board. Not that that would worry the types that do this sort of thing. Look at all the terrorist outrages. Just too bad if old grannies and kids in prams get blown up as well as soldiers or police.'

'Aren't we overlooking a much simpler possibility?' Pollard said tactfully. 'Somebody digging something out that had got embedded in the tyre?'

'If it was obvious enough to spot and worth taking the trouble to get it out, wouldn't Railsdon have seen it himself?' Toye queried.

'Not necessarily. Spotting it would be a matter of luck, depending on how far the wheel turns as you draw up. We'd better see Railsdon after the funeral this afternoon and find out if the Hyperion's been under cover for any length of time here in Shirborough, or in Mallingham. It's not the sort of job anybody could get away with in a public car park, for instance.'

'It was in dock after Raymond's death for minor repairs to the radiator that she'd bashed against the door. Railsdon goes to the Central Garage in Mallingham,' Blair said.

'Thanks. We'll follow that up.' Pollard glanced at his watch. 'Time for a spot of grub before going over to Loxford. Join us, Inspector? Good. And thanks to you two once again for a first-rate job.' A pound note crackled. 'Have one on us.'

Over a snack and a drink in a nearby pub, Pollard returned to the successful tracing of Basil Railsdon's abortive telephone calls to Pamela Hookway, his part-time typist.

'That was stout work, too,' he said. 'As far as I can see, Railsdon's in the clear, at least as far as direct responsibility for Raymond's death goes. How did you get on to it in the end?'

'We had a bit of luck there. As I said, it was a block of new flats, and it being summer people had their windows open. There's a retired couple below Miss Hookway, and they told our chap her phone's no end of a nuisance. She's self-employed and works at home, you see. They noticed Railsdon's two calls as he kept at it and they realised she must be out. They'd gone out themselves by the time our chap got there, but he found out about them and hung around till they came back. That's why we were late ringing you.'

As Pollard remarked to Toye afterwards, a peaceful snack on their own would have been preferable, but Blair was a decent bloke and far from resenting their take-over, except at the very start, had been extremely friendly and cooperative. Gratified at being asked to join them he admitted his initial disappointment.

'But I'm thankful enough now that the C.C. and the Super decided to pass the buck,' he said, 'and that's a fact. One complication, or maybe red herring, after another, and the list of possible suspects thinning out all the time. If I'm not speaking out of turn, Sir, did you pick up anything in Medstone about the deceased?'

'Mainly what we could have done without,' Pollard replied. 'Statements from the hard-headed manager of the big department store where she'd been working under him for the past ten years. He was emphatic about her level-headedness and competence in a crisis, for one thing. Quoted an example of a fire on her floor. And he told us she was physically strong: capable of heaving whacking great parcels of stock about. Of course none of this adds up to conclusive proof but it does make the panic theory look doubtful, especially as the solicitor's opinion of her temperament and physique was along the same lines. Then another bit of information we picked up was that she had discussed the possible market value of her house with the solicitor, which suggests that she was at least thinking about selling it. Amanda Railsdon told us that when she was taking Raymond round the grounds she was very interested in Abbey Cottage, and asked if she – Amanda – and her future husband were actually going to live in it. She also enquired if Railsdon owned cottages in the village. I'm as certain as one can be without actual proof that Raymond had unearthed some means of blackmailing Railsdon into letting her come and establish herself on his doorstep and flaunt the relationship.'

From this the conversation turned naturally to Railsdon's alibi, until Blair announced with regret that he was due on duty in ten minutes, and departed with assurances that he would be kept up to date on any fresh developments.

'Well, there doesn't seem any point in hanging about here,' Pollard said. 'The only thing we've got lined up is talking to Railsdon about that tyre, and at the moment he's entertaining Webster to lunch. Let's push off and go over to Loxford. We can fill in time looking at the church until the funeral party turns up at three.'

Toye, a firm believer in steady routine work, had been on the point of suggesting a further study of the case file, but a glance at the worried look on Pollard's face made him change his mind and remark that he could do with a breath of fresh air himself.

It was a close and stuffy August afternoon. The hedgerows along the Shirborough-Mallingham road were white and dusty, and the branches of the trees seemed weighed down by limp foliage. They parked in the gravel sweep on the north side of Loxford church and walked across to the churchyard. A neat pile of fresh earth beside a small excavation lined with greenery awaited Laura Raymond's ashes.

'Near the family graves but not too near,' Pollard commented, reading the inscriptions on some of the neighbouring gravestones. 'This would be her father's, judging by the date. Let's go inside the church. It'll be cooler in there.'

Toye, although an ex-churchwarden in his home parish, had little interest in church history and architecture as a general rule, but Pollard's account of Jeremy Crabbe's detective work in connection with the grave in the chancel formerly believed to be Aretê Overton's evoked his admiration. They stood looking down at the stone.

'You'd never think they could've got away with it,'

195

he said, referring to the nuns of Loxford Abbey. 'That Abbess must've been quite a character . . . They've made a nice job of getting the stone back and mending that crack running right across. The mortar was matched up so well you hardly notice it.'

After they had looked at some of the memorials around the walls of the chancel, mainly to deceased members of the Legge family, Toye wandered round looking for evidence of the efficiency or otherwise with which the parish was run. Pollard strolled to the west end. As he turned to look up at the west window his eye was caught by the display of parish magazines and other literature arranged on a table below it. A brightly-coloured pamphlet carried a sketch of the exterior of the church on the cover and the legend '*St Mary's, Loxford. Our Tower Appeal*'. It seemed to be offered free, but he dropped ten pence into the box on the table before taking a copy and sitting down in one of the back pews to study it.

The author was Martin Crabbe, M.A. Oxon, Vicar of St Mary's, Loxford, and it had been printed in March of the previous year.

It began with a brief account of the history of the church. A small Norman church of the late tenth century had originally occupied the site of the present building, but all trace of it had vanished. In 1120 Loxford Abbey was founded for a community of Cistercian nuns, and the original church demolished and replaced by a larger one which formed part of the Abbey buildings. The community had apparently flourished, and in the early fifteenth century the church was enlarged and largely rebuilt in the perpendicular style, although a good deal of the Norman stone was incorporated into the nave walls, and was particularly noticeable, Martin Crabbe informed his readers, at the west end of the south wall.

196

Pollard broke off to see for himself, and spent a few interested minutes examining the area to his satisfaction.

'At the time of this rebuilding,' the pamphlet continued, 'the community took a rather daring step to make the Abbey church more impressive. They added a tower. Such an addition was considered to be contrary to the Cistercian ideal of simplicity and the tower was a discreetly modest affair, very little higher than the church roof, and in only two stages. They built it on the north side where it stands to this day, forming the lower part of our present tower. Perhaps unfortunately, the nuns did not stop at that. Fifty years later a third stage was added, together with some more impressive pinnacles, and it is this addition that is causing us, the Loxford parishioners, such a headache four hundred years later. If you go outside and study the uppermost stage of the tower carefully, you will notice that the stone is crumbling alarmingly, especially on the south and west sides. An even closer look will show you that it is slightly different in character from the stone used for the two lower stages. It looks rather as though the increase in the tower's height was achieved on the cheap. The diocesan architect has called in expert advice, and the upshot is that we have to find £20,000 as soon as possible for extensive treatment of the stonework and the reconstruction of one of the pinnacles. As the parish knows only too well, our much-loved bells have had to be silenced, as the vibration caused by ringing them would be a potential danger to the tower in its present state. They will be permanently silenced unless we can put the tower to rights, and in the last resort we might have to remove the upper stage altogether in the interests of public safety.

'I know that numerous local money-raising plans have been made, and some are already operational, and we

197

have had exceedingly generous donations from individuals. But £20,000 is a lot of money. We cannot expect the Preservation of Historic Churches authorities to pay a substantial proportion of the bill: they have endless demands on their resources, so – VISITORS PLEASE HELP US IF YOU CAN. *There is a box for contributions by the south door through which you came in.*

'*I shall insert a typed statement of the Appeal's progress in this pamphlet after next year's Annual General Meeting of the parish in March.*

'*Martin Crabbe, Vicar.*'

Pollard studied the statement with interest. Astonishingly, over £10,000 had been raised, including £3,000 from the Preservation of Historic Churches Fund. There were some large individual donations, including one of £1,000 from Basil Railsdon, but a surprising sum had come from coffee mornings, barbecues, jumble sales and similar activities. Martin Crabbe had commented on some of these, including the sponsored marathon to Shirborough Town Hall and back on New Year's Day, and the Musical Evening arranged by the People's Warden, Mr Cobbledick.

'*We always feel proud when our choir is asked to sing Evensong in the Cathedral during the Choir School's summer holiday,*' Martin Crabbe wrote, '*but unfortunately not all of us can manage to get there to hear them. Bill Cobbledick, our People's Warden, is, alongside his many other skills, a lover of music and has sung in the Loxford choir man and boy. This past year he had the splendid idea of getting permission from the Dean to take his fine cassette recorder and player along and tape the choir's sung Evensong. Back here in our own church he fixed up a couple of loud-speakers and played us the recording. It was so excellent that it was difficult to believe that the singing was not coming to us direct from*

198

Mallingham Cathedral . . .'

Pollard sat completely immobile, the thin slip of typing-paper steady in his hand. He had had similar experiences before, moments of sudden illumination in which his bodily existence seemed suspended. Then came the sound of an approaching car, quickly followed by two others. Tyres crunched on gravel as they drew up. Toye's footsteps came echoing down the aisle.

'We'd better go along,' Pollard heard a voice say, hardly recognisable as his own.

Toye took one look at him and followed without speaking.

Outside a small group of people was standing hesitantly beside the cars. A moment later Martin Crabbe gave a lead by starting off in the direction of the churchyard, Bill Cobbledick in an official black suit at his side, bearing the casket containing Laura Raymond's ashes. Basil Railsdon walked behind them with Henrietta Legge on his right carrying a spray of roses and John Webster on his left. Jeremy Crabbe and Amanda brought up the rear, hand-in-hand. After a discreet interval Pollard and Toye followed, Pollard conscious of discomfort in the role of an official presence at an intimate and personal occasion. They remained as unobtrusively as possible in the background.

Bill Cobbledick dropped on one knee and carefully placed the casket in the place prepared for it. He got to his feet again and drew back a little, his expression impassive. The others moved closer. A man in working clothes watched the proceedings from a distance, waiting for the moment when he could begin to replace the earth and the green turf which he had removed during the morning. Martin Crabbe, wearing his cassock, stood apart, looking down at the grave.

199

'Eternal rest give unto her, O Lord,' he said simply and clearly, 'and let perpetual light shine upon her. Amen.'

Pollard had a sudden, fleeting sense of Laura Raymond's death having moved into some totally different context. He saw Henrietta Legge stoop to place the spray of roses by the side of the grave and exchange a swift glance with Martin Crabbe. Basil Railsdon slipped his arm through hers and there was a general movement in the direction of the church. Pollard and Toye went quickly ahead and stationed themselves beside the Rover. After arranging for Amanda to drive Henrietta back to Abbey Cottage he came across to them.

'Did you want me, Chief Superintendent?' he asked Pollard. 'I've just got to run Mr Webster into Shirborough for the London train, but I'll be coming straight back to the house, if you can wait. Mrs Bennett will be there if you'd like to make use of the study, or there are chairs on the lawn.'

'Thank you,' Pollard said. 'We'll go up. We've got some information about that tyre that you should have.'

The Hyperion drove off rapidly. Amanda Railsdon's car had already left. Through the churchyard gate could be seen the figures of Martin Crabbe, Bill Cobbledick and the workman, engaged in conversation.

'We'll drive up to the house right away,' Pollard said tersely. 'Bill Cobbledick killed her. I know in broad outline how, but God alone knows why.'

Toye's hand halted fractionally on the point of inserting the ignition key, but otherwise his habitual self-control held. As they progressed up the drive of Loxford House Pollard told him to park near the beginning of the path leading to the feedstore.

200

'Don't make more row than you can help,' he added. 'At all costs we mustn't get embroiled with Mrs Bennett. Railsdon won't take long over the Shirborough trip.'

In another minute they had drawn up. Pollard took the Tower Appeal pamphlet out of his pocket and extracted the typewritten slip on which Martin Crabbe had summarised the first year's fund-raising results.

Toye perused it twice before turning his head and looking at Pollard with incredulous admiration.

'Come off it, for God's sake,' Pollard said angrily. 'Why the hell didn't we consider the possibility of Cobbledick before?'

'Because of all the evidence that he was working up on the roof,' Toye retorted with unusual vigour, 'and because it simply doesn't add up. Cobbledick can't have set eyes on Raymond before, unless he passed her in the street when she was down at Easter, or coming back here in the Hyperion from the station on the Tuesday afternoon. All right, motive's a dirty word on an investigation, but in this job there's either got to be a credible one or it's a case of diminished responsibility which will hardly stick, I'd have thought.'

Pollard looked at his watch.

'Well anyway, we've got to put motive on one side for the moment and concentrate on means. Come on. I want to get round to the stable block and see how this cassette player loud-speaker gear could have been rigged up. Luckily Bennett's sitting-room where she's probably enjoying a cuppa doesn't look out at the back.'

They left the car and took the track through the trees which brought them out in the stable yard. The former stables had been divided into three garages and a smaller section at the far end. All the debris from the re-roofing had been cleared up and the interior of the garages freshly whitewashed. They had tip-up doors and overhead strip lighting which could be switched on and off from just inside. The first was unlocked but completely empty. The doors of the second and third had been left up, presumably for returning cars.

'Railsdon's and Amanda's,' Pollard said, moving on to the last section. This had a door of the ordinary type. There was an old-fashioned key in the lock which turned easily and they went in to find a small workshop with a bench under an east-facing window. It was fitted up with an assortment of the tools in use in the average household and those needed by car-owners to carry out minor repairs and adjustments. Here, too, there was overhead strip lighting, and also a couple of power points over the bench. Pollard and Toye stood looking at them in silence.

'So that's how it was done,' Pollard said.

'Leads running down from a cassette recorder-player and an amplifier up on the roof.'

'Yes. Through this window. First stage: tape yourself working normally on a re-roofing job. Bursts of hammering with intervals while you place the next batten in position. Entirely authentic sounds stored in the cassette ready for when you want them. On D-day plug in the lead from the amplifier and connect with the recorder. Slip in your cassette. You will have already tested for volume in some other place. At the moment of blast-off, simply depress the PLAY key.'

'How about fixing the gear on a sloping roof like this one?'

'No problem really. Cobbledick's a builder and used to working on roofs. One solution could be a couple of ladders lashed together, the lower one running up from ground level and the other lying flat on the slope of the roof. And one often sees small platforms of planks supported by some scaffolding. Easy enough to secure the record-player and the amplifier to either of these with a bit of ingenuity. And remember that up to the time of Raymond's death Cobbledick was working on the north side. This was a vital part of the scheme, of course.'

'I'll give you all that,' Toye conceded, 'but what about timing? You couldn't fix up all this overnight. How did Cobbledick know Raymond was coming down and that she'd be going to the feedstore to get the car that morning? Why on earth did he want to murder her, anyway?'

It was oppressively close and silent in the little workshop, and the smell of oil and metal hung in the air. With his back to the window Pollard leant against the bench, his hands gripping its edge. His eyes met Toye's.

'He didn't,' he said. 'He probably didn't even know she existed. The penny's just dropped. Cobbledick was out to murder Railsdon.'

*   *   *

In the privacy of the Rover they worked out a possible sequence of events on the Wednesday morning when Laura Raymond had met her death in the feedstore. From his own account Bill Cobbledick had in the past done a number of building jobs at Loxford House, and would be familiar with Basil Railsdon's morning routine. How he took in the mail on its arrival at about nine-thirty, took his letters to the study and spent a varying amount of time dealing with them. Sooner or later he would emerge, get his car and go out.

'What I think happened was this,' Pollard went on,

'Cobbledick knew Railsdon's routine and acted accordingly. Soon after he heard the mail van drive off at about a couple of minutes after nine-thirty, he stopped working, set the cassette playing and nipped down to wait behind the feedstore. To fit in with the evidence of the Tremlett-Browns, Raymond would have come along at twenty to ten or just after, opened up, and got into the car. If the T-Bs had looked out of that cottage window fractionally earlier they would probably have noticed her. After taking a look at the controls she would have tried her hand at starting up the Hyperion's engine, the signal for Cobbledick to run round and shut and secure the door. All right! You needn't bother to ask why she didn't switch off again immediately, old man. I'm pretty sure she did.'

Light slowly dawned in Toye's absorbed face.

'Meaning he got carbon monoxide into the place from outside? He had a van up in the yard, of course . . . He said he'd stopped off earlier on to pick up the weathercock . . .'

'This is almost certainly where the carbon monoxide must have come from I think. He'd probably have left the van behind the feedstore with a handy length of rubber tubing on board, and carried the weathercock up to the stable block. Mrs Bennett would have been having her own breakfast and most unlikely to notice that he'd arrived on foot.'

'But those gratings are bunged right up with dust and dead leaves.'

'Something more purpose-built would have been dreamed up by a chap like Cobbledick, don't you think? A brick taken out of the back wall, and temporarily replaced with one with a hole of just the right diameter to take the rubber tubing fixed on to the exhaust of the van. Then the original brick replaced afterwards.

We've got to spot where it was done. It may be difficult. Remember how well the mortar was matched up round the gravestone in the church?'

'It's an old building. The difference would show under analysis.'

'First find your brick,' Pollard retorted. 'The Shirborough technicians will cope, of course, but the last thing we can afford to do at the moment is to alert Cobbledick by turning up here with a brace of lab chaps draped in their equipment . . . Reverting to our step-by-step reconstruction of Cobbledick's activities that morning: he must have set another instalment of the cassette going, and slipped over to the feedstore again to rig the scene to look like an accident. He'd have unfastened the door and had the most appalling shock. Instead of Railsdon sprawled out with the high colour and blue lips of carbon monoxide poisoning, he'd be greeted by the sight of a woman he'd probably never seen before lying dead on the floor. But he kept his head, didn't he? Switched on the Hyperion's engine, left the door unfastened and went back to the stables in his van with the rubber tubing hidden in it. No one seeing him arrive would think twice about the van. They'd assume he'd been to fetch something. He'd park in a handy position for stowing away the cassette player and the amplifier, and carry on with the roof job . . . All we've got to do now is to find out why Cobbledick had it in for Railsdon.'

'Coming up the drive,' Toye interposed hastily.

'Hell! How he must have scorched. Well, the agenda of the moment is simply and solely his damaged tyre, of course.'

Basil Railsdon emerged from the Hyperion looking almost buoyant.

'Sorry to have kept you hanging about,' he said. 'Do

205

come in. Webster got his train all right. He's prepared to cope with Laura's estate once the adjourned inquest proceedings are over. A very decent chap, I thought. Tell me about this tyre business,' he went on as they settled down in the study. 'What did the forensic lab make of the damage?'

'Before we get on to that,' Pollard replied, 'I'm glad to be able to tell you that those two unanswered telephone calls you made to Miss Hookway last Wednesday week have been confirmed. She lives in a block of flats, and the rather longer than normal rings were noticed by a couple downstairs at approximately the times you think you made them.'

He watched Basil Railsdon's face narrowly as he spoke, and saw satisfaction but nothing that could be interpreted as profound relief.

'Thanks for letting me know that, Chief Superintendent,' Basil said. 'Can I take it, then, that I'm no longer a suspect where my half-sister's death is concerned?'

'We're satisfied that it was physically impossible for you to have killed her,' Pollard assured him. 'Now to go on to the matter of the damaged tyre. Neither we nor Shirborough are satisfied about this. Their technicians have put in a lot of work on it. Photographs show beyond any doubt that the damage couldn't have been accidental. A groove has been enlarged with a sharp knife, and below this a hole has been gouged out almost down to the canvas. Sooner or later you were bound to pick up something sharp which would work its way down and penetrate the inner tube, and the technicians have extracted a nail.

'Good Lord!' Basil Railsdon looked completely bewildered. 'What on earth does it add up to? I mean, it's a pretty inefficient way of bumping anybody off, isn't it? No control over the time and the place. And

206

vandals go for quick results so that they can watch the fun . ... It's appalling when you come to think about it. I often have my daughter in the car with me, and Miss Legge, and any visitors who may be staying with us.'

'I absolutely agree with all that,' Pollard replied. 'The only other suggestion that the technicians have come up with is that you drove over something that partly penetrated the outer covering of the tyre but still showed, and looked valuable enough for some crook to gouge out. A gold tiepin or brooch, for instance.'

As he spoke he thought he saw fleeting anxiety in Basil Railsdon's eyes, but was unsure.

'Well, it's a possibility of course. It's easy enough to pick up something without knowing it. But if it was obvious enough to attract the notice of a thief, surely I should have spotted it myself? I run my eye over my tyres almost as a matter of routine to see if the pressure looks O.K. But on the other hand one doesn't see the whole tyre at one go.'

'Another point, Sir,' Toye contributed, 'is that the job would have taken quite a bit of time. It was carefully done. Nobody would have risked it in a town car park, for instance. Can you think of any fairly secluded but accessible place where your car has been left recently?'

'It's been in dock at my Mallingham garage, the Central, to have the superficial damage to the radiator dealt with, but they're most reliable people, and I know the whole place is locked up after working hours. Anyway, if there'd been a break-in I should have heard about it. Of course there's no lock on the door of the feedstore, and the car was there while Cobbledick was working on the stable block, but I simply can't imagine anyone from the village either having spotted anything stuck in one of the tyres or slinking up here to dig it out.'

'I suppose we'll have to call it a day, then,' Pollard said. 'It's on the books, though, and Shirborough will be on the watch for any more developments of the same sort.'

As he saw them out Basil Railsdon remarked that life really had been a bit much of late.

'Now that we all seem to be off the hook I shall insist on a weekend break in London for the family four-some,' he said. 'We could all do with a decent hotel and a show tomorrow night, and something pleasant and not too exacting on Sunday.'

* * *

On returning to Shirborough police station Pollard was informed that Inspector Blair was engaged, but sent in an urgent message asking to see him as soon as possible. A quarter of an hour later Blair arrived apologetically in the Yard's temporary office with an enquiring expression.

'This Raymond case has suddenly been stood on its head,' Pollard told him. 'We feel we've been on the wrong track from the word go. Briefly, we've come to the conclusion that Raymond was (a) killed by Cobble-dick the builder, but (b) by mistake. The intended victim was Railsdon. Do you know of any reason why Cobbledick should want to murder Railsdon? We're satisfied that he had the means and the opportunity to do it, but unless the chap's round the bend he must have had a motive of some sort.'

Blair stifled an exclamation.

'Did you hear anything about the disappearance of a little kid from a holiday camp between here and Lox-ford a couple of months ago?' he asked.

Both Pollard and Toye replied that they had heard

about it from the media and the press at the time, and it had been mentioned by various people since they came down to the area, and they had learnt that the child was Bill Cobbledick's grand-daughter.

'You'll have noticed a minor road going off on the right on the main road between here and Loxford, about three miles from here. It's the old coast road. Narrow and undulating and winding, but it's a short-cut. The holiday camp belongs to a farm between this coast road and the main road. The little girl was thought at first to have wandered off on her own, and crossed this road and ended up falling over the cliff. We laid on a search in a big way, and had an S.O.S. put on the evening regional news asking anyone who'd been on the coast road at the time concerned to contact us. Several did, and one of them was Basil Railsdon. He was selected as the Tory candidate for this constituency that morning, here at the Party Committee Rooms, and drove back to Loxford afterwards to be in on the opening of that tomb in Loxford Church. He was a bit late and took the coast road to save time. He stated that he hadn't seen any other vehicle on it. I visited all the people who'd rung in, and he confirmed and signed his statement. In the end we called off the search, and the kid's body's never been found.'

They sat in silence for a few moments.

'Naturally,' Pollard said, 'you searched the coast road for any sign of an accident?'

'Searched it with a toothcomb, Sir, and didn't find a sign of anything. Several things didn't help. The kid had been missing for several hours before the alarm was given because of a mix-up at the camp. Then there was a heavy shower just after midday which could have washed out skid marks and whatever . . . If I might express an opinion, Sir, I think perhaps the Super ought to come in on this.'

209

'So do I,' Pollard replied. 'In fact I was just going to suggest it myself.'

Superintendent Gregg's reaction was decisive. He put through a call to the Chief Constable, and at six o'clock Pollard gave his reconstruction of Laura Raymond's death to a rivetted audience.

'Don't get me wrong,' he ended. 'At the moment we've no definite proof of by far the greater part of all this. I can only say that it appears to meet the known facts. And this information about Railsdon having been on the coast road in a powerful car at that time strikes one as suggestive.'

The Shirborough men agreed.

'If Railsdon's found to have run down that kid and somehow got rid of the body, there's going to be a worse stink than if he'd killed his half-sister,' Major Freeman remarked gloomily. 'However. What help can we lay on in the search for proof, Mr Pollard?'

'We'd like to borrow your technicians to see if they can locate a recently-replaced brick in the back of the feedstore, and to take samples of the mortar, and of the mortar at various other points. Analysis will show any differences of age and composition. Basil Railsdon intends to take his daughter and her fiancé, Jeremy Crabbe, and Miss Legge to London tomorrow for a bit of a let-up, so the coast should be clear tomorrow afternoon. We'd be along, too, and I thought I'd try chatting up the housekeeper a bit.'

'What about?' enquired Superintendent Gregg.

'Basil Railsdon's movements from roughly lunchtime onwards on the day the kid vanished. She probably won't be able to remember with any accuracy, but I think it's worth trying. If he ran over the kid, what did he do with the body? As we know, permanent conceal-ment's damn difficult, and up to now he's been outstandingly successful. On timing he must, I think, have brought it back to Loxford in his car. He could hardly have got rid of it *en route*. So early next week I'm proposing to chat up everybody who was actually present at the tomb-opening in the church. Except, of course, Cobbledick and his workmen. Having got the mortar samples, I thought I'd go back to London and drop them in at the Yard. No reflection on your admirable chaps here, but our equipment is probably a bit better.'

'Understatement of the year,' commented Superintendent Gregg drily.

'Well, you delivered the goods over that tyre of Railsdon's all right. By the way, it crossed my mind just now that those scraps of plastic might possibly have come from something the kid was wearing. I expect you've got a description of everything she had on that day?'

Blair went off in search of the Pippa Cobbledick file. He returned in a short time and began to work methodically through its contents.

'Here's the list,' he said. 'She – ' He broke off suddenly and looked at Pollard with undisguised admiration. 'She had had her ears pierced and was wearing a pair of small, blue plastic earrings,' he read aloud.

Pollard broke a slightly uncomfortable silence by remarking that the jackpot did come up once in a while if you kept at it long enough.

'I'd better take that little lot along too,' he said.

*   *   *

The visit to Loxford House with the technicians was fixed for three o'clock on the following afternoon, by which time it seemed safe to assume that Basil Railsdon and his party would have left for London. On arrival

211

Pollard directed his workforce to the feedstore and rang the front door bell. High-pitched barking was audible. After a brief interval he was aware of being scrutinised from a window, and a moment later bolts were shot back, and a key turned. The door was opened by Mrs Bennett who looked almost pleased to see him.

'You'll think I'm an old fuss-pot,' she said, 'but I'm not all that keen on being here on my own these days, and Mr Railsdon's had special bolts put on all the ground-floor doors. He's gone off to London with Miss Legge and Miss Amanda and young Mr Crabbe.'

Pollard assured her that he only wished that everyone alone in a house was as sensible as she was.

'I only looked in to tell you that I've brought over a couple of science workers to make an investigation in the feedstore,' he explained. 'I was afraid you might see them and wonder what they were up to.'

'Very considerate of you, Sir,' she said. 'Won't you come inside while you're waiting for them? We'll leave the door open and Rollo can run in and out. He wants more exercise than I can find time to give him. Down, Rollo.'

The young Labrador who had been sniffing excitedly at Pollard's trousers shot out like a bolt. Sitting beside Mrs Bennett, it was not difficult to steer the conversation in the direction of recent traumatic events, starting with the opening of Areté Overton's grave which she said she couldn't approve of.

'Of course the news that poor little Pippa Cobbledick had disappeared during the day must have been so distressing,' Pollard suggested.

'To think of a thing like that happening down in this part of the world,' Mrs Bennett replied. 'You can hardly credit it, can you? And she's never been found, poor mite. No, I'll never forget that night. Mr Railsdon came in very late for his supper. After eleven o'clock it was. He'd driven the vicar into Mallingham with that gold casket they found. And even at that hour he didn't seem hungry. Tired out with all the upset, and having been to that meeting in the morning about him standing for Parliament at the next election . . .'

He had painlessly acquired the information he wanted, and keeping the conversation flowing was no problem, but he sat with an ear cocked for the return of Toye and the technicians. He heard them approaching sooner than he expected, and after helping Mrs Bennett to recapture Rollo made his farewell and boarded the Rover.

'No problem, Sir,' Sergeant Thirsk told him. 'We'd expected to find it low down because of the car exhaust pipe, and it was tucked away behind a clump of grass and stuff. You could see the difference in the mortar almost at a glance. Inspector Toye's got the samples in clean labelled envelopes.'

'Stout work,' Pollard approved. 'You'll both curse me for wrecking your Saturday afternoon, but I want to stop off for not more than ten minutes at the Vicarage.'

'Overtime,' they reminded him cheerfully.

Martin Crabbe was gardening in his shirtsleeves. Pollard expressed surprise.

'I thought I'd find you writing your sermon for tomorrow.'

'I'm a compulsive getter-ahead, you know,' Martin Crabbe told him. 'My wife always says I'd have been intolerable as a woman: excessively houseproud and punctual. What can I do for you?'

'Just give me one small bit of information. What time did you and Mr Railsdon get back here from Mallingham after you'd deposited the casket with the Cathedral authorities that night?'

'Let me think . . . It was very late. We simply couldn't

213

get away from them. I remember now: just after half past nine. I was anxious to be back for the ten o'clock news, forgetting that Basil has a car radio. I don't run to luxuries like that. We asked him to stay to supper, but he said Mrs Bennett would have something waiting for him and he'd better get home.'

At Shirborough police station Sergeant Thirsk and Constable May were set down with instructions to report to Inspector Blair, and Pollard and Toye set off on the London road.

'Let's say Railsdon left the Vicarage at a quarter to ten that night,' Pollard said. 'It would leave him roughly an hour to get rid of Pippa Cobbledick's body. The obvious deduction is that he buried it on his own property, somewhere in the Loxford House grounds, but I can see some obvious snags, can't you?'

'He could have parked the Hyperion far enough down the drive to be out of sight from the house,' Toye suggested. 'Nobody'd be likely to be calling at that hour. Then he'd have needed a spade. I noticed what looked like a tool-shed to the right of the drive, up near the Abbey Farm boundary fence. But he'd hardly have risked digging a grave in a cultivated part of the garden. They must employ a gardener the way the place is kept up, and it would be discovered sooner or later. And the alternative'd be going up into the woods behind the house and having to break up hard ground. It would take a lot more than an hour, let alone fetching the body.'

'I suppose it's possible he kept the body locked in the boot overnight and took it off somewhere the next day,' Pollard said, sounding dissatisfied.

They discussed various other possibilities at some length but none sounded convincing. Finally they turned to their immediate plans.

'We'll drop in the stuff at the Yard for the lab boys,'

214

Pollard decided, 'and I'll get the earliest appointment I can with the A.C. on Monday. I'll ask the lab to ring me at home when they've done the tests. Meanwhile let's relax in the company of our nearest and dearest like normal human beings.'

The senior forensic scientist on duty rang Pollard on Sunday evening. The two samples of mortar had been subject to a variety of tests and showed marked differences. One had been exposed to weathering for a long period and had greatly deteriorated.

'If it's part of a building the sooner they get on to some repointing the better,' the scientist said. 'The other sample's quite new. It hasn't dried off long and is finer-grained. There are some small streaks in it of a darker brown mortar, as if whoever put it on hadn't cleaned off the stuff on his trowel from his last job . . . Any use? . . . Hey, are you still there?'

Pollard, whose mind had travelled at the speed of light to the repaired crack in the Overton gravestone, hastily replied that he was.

'Just rather intrigued,' he said. 'What about those bits of what Shirborough say is some sort of plastic?'

'They are plastic. A thin, fragile sort. Pity you couldn't have brought along a bigger sample, but we agree that one piece at any rate was part of a small curved surface, like a bead. What's all this in aid of? This Crantshire case you're on?'

'Yes. Watch this column for the next enthralling instalment.'

'Glad we've been able to help you out of an impasse.'

They exchanged a few more friendly insults before ringing off.

*　　　*　　　*

The following morning Pollard's Assistant Commissioner listened with an apparent lack of serious attention to a resumé of the situation at Loxford.

'Fortunate that you restrained yourself from jumping the gun and arresting this Railsdon chap for murdering the woman,' he commented. 'What do you propose to do next?'

'Go back to Loxford, Sir, and find out from the vicar exactly how the grave was left overnight after the day when it was opened up and the child disappeared.'

'And if it was only partly closed up again, and the child's body could have been put in and been unnoticeable,' the A.C. – who had not missed a trick – pursued, 'you are assuming that Railsdon did the job?'

'Yes, Sir.'

'You realise, I suppose, that the Home Office has already sanctioned one opening of that grave this summer? If they agree to another we shall look pretty good fools if no human remains are found. Imagine the press headlines!'

Pollard conceded that an element of risk was involved.

'All right then, but God help you if there's nothing there. I suppose we shall have to lay on manpower as usual?'

'I think it's essential to avoid bringing any locals in. It might get round, and two Loxford people are involved. Cobbledick as well as Railsdon.'

'Well, get down there at once, and find out what you want to know from the vicar. Ring back if he's prepared to swear that the child's body could have been put into the grave that night, and I'll get on to the Home Office.'

'Thank you, Sir.' Pollard beat a hasty retreat. He found a note on his desk from Toye to say that he was

216

waiting in the Rover, ready to start. He made a brief telephone call to Martin Crabbe and went down in the lift to the car park.

By lunch-time he had left an appalled and shattered Martin Crabbe who had unhesitatingly supplied the necessary information for the exhumation order to be applied for. At Shirborough he brought a gloomily resigned Superintendent Gregg up to date after putting through a call to the Assistant Commissioner's office. During the afternoon he drove back to London with Toye.

The exhumation order came through on Tuesday morning. Thereafter a detailed plan of action was drawn up for Wednesday evening by means of constant telephoning between the Yard and Shirborough police station. Pollard had a lengthy conversation with Martin Crabbe. It was agreed that Jeremy must be told about the re-opening of Aretê Overton's grave but nothing about Basil Railsdon's almost certain involvement in Pippa Cobbledick's death. Because of his engagement to Amanda the information would put him in an intolerable position during the next thirty-six hours. For practical reasons Erica Crabbe would be kept in ignorance to the same extent.

The timetable was determined by the need to arrive at the church without attracting local attention if this were possible. Fortunately it was at the far end of the village. Zero hour was fixed for ten-thirty on Wednesday night. At that hour few Loxford villagers were likely to be about. It would be essential to carry out the work with the minimum of artificial lighting as it was impossible to black out the church windows.

Pollard and Toye left London at six-thirty, approaching Loxford from Mallingham to avoid passing along the village street, and driving straight to the Vicarage

217

where the Rover was parked out of sight from passersby. They arrived at a quarter to nine, and had supper with the Crabbes.

Time crawled, but shortly after ten the four men went over to the church, entering by the south door which Martin Crabbe relocked. Once his eyes became accustomed to the dimness inside, Pollard was struck by the apparent vastness of the interior. The nave appeared boundless. Only the distant chancel illuminated by the rays of the rising moon had its familiar appearance. As he sat down with the others in a pew near the door he felt, to his discomfiture, both the hunter's exhilaration and hideous qualms of doubt. It was warm inside the church, and the air was charged with a composite smell of flowers, old stone and books. The faint, stealthy sounds of an old building were audible. Only Jeremy appeared at ease, protected by his interest in this further instalment in the long history of Aretê Overton's grave.

After a time conversation flagged. There were lengthy silences broken by the shifting of someone's position and an occasional clearing of a throat. At long last cars were heard approaching from the main road, gravel scrunching under their wheels. The sound of braking followed. Martin Crabbe unlocked the south door and all four men went outside. Superintendent Gregg and Inspector Blair emerged from one car with two constables, the Home Office representative and a police doctor from another, and three workmen with a variety of equipment from the third. There was a brief preliminary discussion and the cars were driven round to the east end of the church.

'Park out of sight of the road, and don't use your lights unless you must,' Pollard said. 'You can see the back of the church from Railsdon's place.'

218

As soon as the drivers had returned Martin Crabbe re-locked the south door and there was a general move to the chancel. The three workmen unpacked their gear, inspected the Aretê Overton gravestone and began operations in the light of two powerful but shaded electric lamps.

The rest of the party settled in the choir stalls. Pollard found himself sitting next to Jeremy Crabbe who commented on the more sophisticated technique being used on this occasion.

'That electric drill's cutting into the mortar round the sides as if it was butter,' he remarked. 'Makes a bit of a row, though doesn't it? The same sort of chisel bars and rollers as old Cobbledick's . . .'

Time passed. Pollard glanced at intervals at the east window, and wondered anxiously if it appeared faintly luminous from Loxton House. Or had Railsdon by a remote chance seen the lights of the cars as they turned in? The workmen at last began the shifting of the gravestone on the rollers. After a few minutes the doctor came down to the onlookers in the choir stalls.'

'You're spot on, Chief Super,' he told Pollard. 'There's a body down there right enough, and a pretty small one. The next stage won't be exactly pleasant.'

He returned and stood beside the Home Office official at the open grave. A ladder was lowered and the foreman of the working party went down. The lamps were focussed downwards. In response to a request, sheets of polythene were passed down. Finally a bundle swathed in these was hoisted to the surface and deposited on the chancel floor. The doctor knelt down to examine the contents. After a further pause he got to his feet again and came towards the police.

'I'll have to carry out a full P.M., of course,' he said, 'but I can tell you straight away that it's the body of a

219

small girl of about three or four. It's dry down there and the state of preservation's pretty good. Her neck and right shoulder are broken. She's wearing a little kid's white shirt, blue shorts and white sandals. Her ears have been pierced and there's a small blue earring on a bit of gold wire in the right ear, but the other one's missing.'

''Tis 'ere,' a hoarse voice said from the doorway into the vestry. 'I got 'un. Dug 'un outer the offside front tyre o' that bastard Railsdon's car.'

In a split second the choir stalls emptied. Shafts of torchlight coming at different angles held trapped the tense figure in rough working clothes now standing in front of the altar with clenched right hand outstretched. Pollard detached himself from the group and went forward.

'William Cobbledick,' he said quietly and authoritatively, 'I hold a warrant for your arrest on a charge of murdering Laura Raymond by subjecting her to carbon monoxide poisoning on Wednesday, August the third. It is my duty to warn you that anything you say may be used in evidence.'

'By God it will!' Bill Cobbledick shouted. 'I can't wait to get to court and tell 'em it wasn't that woman I was out to get. 'Twas that bloody bastard Raiisdon who ran down our Pippa and chucked 'er into that grave there like a dead dog.'

There was a smothered gasp . . . Jeremy, Pollard thought, conscious of regrouping in progress.

'If, as you say, you have that missing earring, Mr Cobbledick,' he said, 'it must be handed over for examination, and may be required as evidence at a later stage.'

'Take 'un then, and you best take back spare's vestry key, Vicar. I shan't 'ave no more use for 'ee. An' I'll

220

come quiet. No need . . .'

He broke off as the strident note of a police siren was suddenly audible, gaining in volume moment by moment. Brakes screamed outside the south door. Martin Crabbe, with Jeremy and Superintendent Gregg on his heels, ran down the aisle to unlock the door on which someone was hammering furiously. The driver of a police car was on the step.

'999 call,' he reported. 'From Loxford House. Mr Railsdon's shot himself.'

Jeremy pushed past, towards the Vicarage and his car, running.

'Step on it,' Gregg ordered, plunging into the car. 'Tell Blair to follow on.'

The car roared off. The church was suddenly flooded with light. For a moment the group in the chancel stood immobilised. The spell was broken by a harsh laugh from Bill Cobbledick.

'So Railsdon's killed 'imself to save 'is face. Stop at nothin' to do that, would 'e?'

Epilogue

From the *North Crantshire Evening News*

INQUEST VERDICTS

On Pippa Ethel Cobbledick of Shirborough:
Death by Misadventure . . .
On Laura Raymond of Medstone, Surrey: Unlaw-
fully killed . . .
On Basil Robert Railsdon of Loxford:
Suicide . . .

COMMITTAL TO THE CROWN COURT

William Cobbledick of Loxford, charged with the
murder of Laura Raymond . . .

*   *   *

From *The Times*

MARRIAGES

CRABBE-RAILSDON – Jeremy Hamlyn
Crabbe, only son of the Reverend M. H. and Mrs

222

Crabbe of Loxford, to Amanda Catherine, only daughter of the late Mr and Mrs Basil Railsdon of Loxford.

*　　*　　*

From *Country Life*
WESTINGFOLD AND PARTNERS
NORTH CRANTSHIRE
Loxford
SHIRBOROUGH 9 miles
An exceptionally attractive mid-Georgian house incorporating earlier features. Fully modernised and in mint condition. Set in extensive gardens and woodland . . . £250,000

*　　*　　*

From the Vicar's letter in St Mary's, Loxford, Parish Magazine

'We are deeply grateful to our Bishop for coming to take our Parish Communion service and talk to us in a very dark hour . . .

'Our congratulations and warmest wishes for the future to Mr and Mrs Jeremy Crabbe on their marriage. All Loxford is delighted that they have bought Pilgrim Cottage to be their permanent home base . . .

'Miss Henrietta Legge and Mr Walter White have been appointed Acting Churchwardens pending formal elections at the Annual Parish Meeting next March . . .

'The Tower Appeal . . .'

If you have enjoyed this mystery and would like to
receive details of other Walker mysteries,
please write to:

Mystery Editor
Walker and Company
720 Fifth Avenue
New York, New York 10019